LEAD
ME
HOME

LEAD
ME
HOME

a novel by

Niles Reddick

Jan-Carol
Publishing, Inc

"every story needs a book"

LEAD ME HOME

All Rights Reserved © 2010 by Niles Reddick
Published February 2010
Second Printing March 2017

RoseHeart Publishing
Imprint of Jan-Carol Publishing, Inc.
Cover Design by CH Creations
Cover Photo by Steven Robinson
Interior Layout and Design by CH Creations

ISBN 13: 978-0-9841870-6-5

You may contact the publisher:
Jan-Carol Publishing, Inc.
PO Box 701
Johnson City, TN 37605
publisher@jancarolpublishing.com
jancarolpublishing.com

Dedicated to my children, Audrey and Nicholas,
and to my wife Michelle.

With appreciation to my mother for reading; to friends Scott
and Meghan and cousins Byron and Charlotte for listening; to
Motlow colleagues, Brenda, Linda, Mary, Jeannette, Susan
and Annette for encouragement, support, and ideas; to old
friends and co-workers from days gone by and to relatives at
rest for inspiration; and to God for the ability.

Through many dangers, toils and snares
I have already come;
'Tis Grace that brought me safe thus far
and Grace will lead me home.

From John Newton's *Amazing Grace*

Chapter
1

Aunt Catfish didn't look right in her casket. The way she had been laid in there made her look like she had no neck, and there were people who had no necks, since I knew a boy in grade school who had no neck. In fact, his whole family had no necks, which was a genetic defect. And I had wondered how doctors reacted to treating that family, if they had to read up on the neckless phenomena prior to treating them for throat problems or glandular issues.

As I looked around the church, people would approach the casket, look in and shake their heads. Some said how good she looked, which always made me feel odd, probably because it wasn't true—no one looks good dead, really—and also because Aunt Catfish didn't look good without her neck. I felt like everyone who had come to the church funeral knew Aunt Catfish because I can usually spot a funeral addict, one who goes to funerals just to socialize, but it had been a year since I'd come home. Catfish wasn't her real name either. It was Ophelia, but I called her Catfish only to myself and my friends and some cousins when I was a child and I trusted them not to tell. The reason I called her Catfish was because she loved to go swimming in the pond—something most of us were afraid of because of alligators and moccasins. She had olive skin that was slick, thin lips, and dark whiskers, just a few. I never understood why she didn't pluck them like her sister-in-law who was my grandmother. I'd watch my grand-mother pluck her whiskers and eyebrows, then paint some new ones on, and she would even paint them higher and in an arch, making Granny look a lot meaner than she honestly was. My daddy and I had the skin color Aunt Catfish had, but he shaved daily, as did I, so neither of us knew if we would've had the whiskers otherwise. Once I made the mistake of tell-ing Mama Aunt Ophelia looked like a catfish and she said, "Shut your filthy mouth, boy." I never said another word, but I suspected Mama thought she looked like a catfish, too.

I really didn't want to leave Tennessee and drive eight hours to the funeral, but I felt obliged. None of my cousins wanted to come either, even though most of them still lived there. In fact, when we would go home for the holidays, they would still expect us to drive around and visit them because they were too busy or lazy to drive a few miles to visit us.

Aunt Catfish's friends stood above her in the choir loft, all dressed in maroon robes, singing "Leaning on the Ever-lasting Arms" followed by "Precious Memories," and I looked at Mama. She was sobbing, and my Daddy was stone-faced and squinting. Each choir member had a handkerchief and they dabbed the corners of their eyes as they sang. I didn't think it sounded as good as on Sundays when I was home for a visit and they sang. I figured it was probably be-cause they were burying their friend. I also imagined they were looking down in the casket and seeing Catfish without her neck, wondering if the funeral director was going to fix them that way and, even more important, wondering if they were next. I didn't think much about death until I had to go to a funeral, but I knew I'd end up that way one day, too. I thought I would worry about that later. There seemed to be too many other things to worry about at the time.

As I glanced around the room, it seemed like everyone from town was present, and that's the way it usually was. People got off work and just walked across the street to the Baptist Church for a funeral. There were also a lot of flowers. The one I thought was the most interesting was the wreath that read "Jesus called" and had a little plastic phone attached. Aunt Catfish would have liked that one because it was the most creative, she would've said, throwing her right hand in the air and saying, "Praise God." She was always saying that about something, whether it was good or bad. I really didn't understand why she would say "Praise God" about someone getting sick or killed, like her three fiancés had, but she did. Her first fiancé had been killed in a car crash, way before I was ever born, but everyone in the family told the story, told how mangled everything was, and how she would pull a box from her cedar chest and look at all the pictures on his birthday. Her second fiancé had caught the flu during the epidemic, went into a coma and never came out. Her third fiancé had been killed in the Korean War, which Catfish would say was the forgotten war. I guess after the third one, she gave up. She lived to be in her nineties. Mama said she wouldn't have lived that long if she'd been married. Catfish lived right by herself on the Tallokas farm just a few miles outside the town of Pavo, Georgia. The town had been named for her granddaddy who set up the first post office, and the Tallokas farm had been in the family since before the Civil War when Catfish's granddaddy and my great granddaddy had received a free grant of land after he came over from Europe.

After "Precious Memories," the choir sang "Farther A-long" acapella, a sad, slow song, and for some reason, I don't know if the song was as cheery as the writer intended.

Since Catfish helped take care of everyone who was sick or dying, having had time because she was what everyone called an old maid, she knew death well. She wasn't a nurse, but she knew a little about what to do, probably from practice. It wasn't uncommon for her to call our house when I was growing up and ask my daddy to come help haul someone to the funeral home, or if the funeral director could come help load the person into the hearse. My daddy is in line to take over the farm, but he's in his seventies and won't. He says he won't sell it, but he's hinted at my moving home and living there, and I can't stop thinking about it. I'd moved to get away, not that I really needed to. In fact, I don't know why I did, now that I think about it, but at the time I needed more, and yet all I can think about now is going home, and even more enticing, there would be no mortgage. Of course, there would be no job either since there are no resorts, or even chain hotels in Pavo. There are some chains and bed and breakfasts in Thomasville, just a short drive from the Tallokas farm.

"And now Aunt Catfish has gone home," the preacher, Reverend Mason, said, all the while mopping sweat beads from his face with a white handkerchief. "Ophelia was ironically killed in a car crash, like her first love, though she wasn't mangled, bless her heart."

The preacher was right. Aunt Catfish wasn't mangled. In fact, when I got the call and learned she collided with a log truck, I figured it would be a closed casket. In reality, the wreck didn't kill her. The impact of her chest on the steering wheel caused wires in her chest from heart surgery twenty years ago to puncture her heart. Aunt Catfish didn't even look like she'd been in a wreck, except I did wonder if the wreck had lowered her neck a bit. Catfish had been in several wrecks in the last few years and probably shouldn't have been driving, but no one had the gumption to tell her so. When she'd drive into town to shop and have a wreck, the police chief would take her to the town jail, but not put her in a cell, then call my daddy who would go get her, take her home, and then have her 1950's Pontiac towed and repaired. I often wondered how she could've had so many wrecks. Everyone could see the thirty-five year old battleship coming down the road, and most who knew her would get out of her way. When I would call home, Mama would say, "Your aunt Ophelia has done gone and had another wreck. She ought not be driving and I've told your daddy, but he won't listen."

"Doesn't she have to take a driver's test?"

"She had it renewed a few years ago and now can do it by mail, so she don't have to take the test."

"How's her health?"

"She's going down. She probably won't be here next year. You ought to come home and visit."

And then the guilty feelings would start and fester in my mind like a mosquito one hears by his ears but can never find to swat. "I'll see if I can get off work." And so, I would make the trek to Georgia and visit everyone and see Aunt Catfish, and every other relative, who all said they were proud I married my high school sweetheart, Jaden, that I had gone to college, got a business degree, moved to Nashville, Tennessee and took a management position with a hotel company downtown. The first year or two after we moved, Jaden and I would send photos of Nashville back home to Mama and Daddy, and her parents, too. They would carry them around and show everyone, particularly if it was someone famous we'd met in Nashville like Brenda Lee, Loretta Lynn, George Jones, or Dolly Parton.

And of course, we'd invite relatives and friends to come visit and we were sincere. The only people who took us up on it, once, were our parents, and when traffic began to get heavy just outside Murfreesboro on I-24, they called from a pay phone, and we had to go get them and one of us drive their car the rest of the way. I was amazed they'd made it that far because they got so nervous in Atlanta and driving over to Monteagle, Daddy had to hear Mama driving from her seat, "Watch that truck!" or "Watch that guard rail!" or "Watch for falling rocks!" She'd grip the door handle and press the floorboard with her foot as if her imaginary pedal would slow their vehicle. They could've flown to Nashville via Atlanta or Tallahassee, but were too paranoid.

Once when Pavo began a yearly festival, the organizer, Emma Mae MacDougal, actually called our condo and left a message. I called her back, excited that someone might be coming to visit, but she wanted me to get one of the famous people we'd met to come perform for the festival in Pavo and judge the country music singing competition. She was disappointed when I explained we didn't personally know them, that we'd only met them at events in town. A day or two later, my mama called and said, "You ought not be passing yourself off for more than you are and getting people's hopes up." Of course, Jaden and I hadn't. We had always explained we were at this event or another just like thousands of others; it was our families who made it out to be more than it was. I suspected Mama was the one who made it out to be more than it was, since she lived in town and made rounds daily to the insurance office, florist, bank, and grocery store. Jaden's parents owned peach orchards and a blueberry farm and didn't go to town much.

After the prayer, the funeral home attendants, solemn in their tight-fitting pin-striped suits and squeaky leather shoes, removed the flower blanket and closed the lid. They turned the casket on its stand with wheels toward the aisle of the church, and deacons from the Baptist church moved slowly to grip the aluminum handles. As they moved forward, the choir broke into "I'll Fly Away," Aunt Catfish's favorite song.

Once the casket rolled out, the rows of people began to empty and file toward the vestibule onto the stoop, finally spilling into the yard, where men stood shifting from one foot to another talking about the heat. Women fanned with cardboard hand-held fans advertising the funeral home, not that it needed advertising since it was the only one, and said what a beautiful service it was. One woman said, "Ophelia would've loved it. I wished she could've seen it."

I walked over to my parents' car, got in, and turned the ignition. I turned the air conditioner on full blast and waited for my parents, who were receiving hugs and condolences all the way down the sidewalk. It was as though the funeral attendees hadn't seen them in years, when in reality it was only two days ago they were in church with them and already Aunt Catfish was dead, lying cold on a metal table at the funeral home.

I needed to go to the restroom, but I knew I would have to wait. I felt I could probably sneak off in the woods by the cemetery when everyone was praying and go. Then again, I imagined Aunt Catfish seeing me, pulling a hickory switch and swatting my behind from relieving myself on her precious lilies. I could hear her raspy voice saying, "Boy, you ain't no dog. Praise God."

My parents slammed their doors, and we followed behind the hearse destined for the isolated cemetery a few miles out in the county. I had played hide and seek behind grave-stones, had played spin the bottle in an unlocked mausoleum, drank beer with friends, busting bottles on headstones, and snatched flowers from arrangements to take to Jaden before we married and moved to Tennessee because I had no money. Each time I went home, memories rushed like waves crashing onto a deserted beach.

"Lord, it's hot. I'm about to burn slam up," Mama said, pulling on the top of her dress several times to cool her chest, even though she didn't pin money to her bra like Granny did. "Max, you okay?"

"Sure, why?"

"You seem distant and you keep weaving from one side of the road to the other. People will think you're drunk or trying to be cute. This is a funeral."

"I'm okay, just thinking. Sorry," I said.

Daddy chimed in. "You thinking of moving and taking over the home place?"

"No," I said. "I was wondering what Jaden is doing."

"Oh, that's so sweet," Mama said. "I wish she could've come. Ophelia would have loved it."

Catfish is dead. She wouldn't have even known. "Yes, Jaden was upset she couldn't get off work, but she couldn't get a substitute."

"Well," Mama said, "there's plenty of substitutes at the school here. She won't have trouble with that if ya'll move back. I'm even still on the list, though things have changed since you were a boy. These kids are into all sorts of things. You know someone was caught busting bottles on graves at the cemetery recently?"

I looked at her quizzically.

"Boy got probation. Should've got more than that, if you ask me." She stared out the window. "Oh, Ophelia would have loved her service. She'd love it more if you could've got some of the Carter family to come sing "Will the Circle Be Unbroken.""

"Mama, I don't know that family. I have seen them and heard them, but I don't know them."

"Well, you ought to. You need to get out more and get to know people. That's how to move up in the world."

I didn't want to move up in the world, really, any more than I already had, but I did entertain the idea of moving home, and though I knew Jaden wanted to move home at some point to help her parents as they aged, part of me just couldn't stomach the thought of her going to teach in the high school where her first boyfriend was the principal. He was married, and yet I feared he still pined for Jaden. Billy Ray had been the football player, the student council president, and he was also a hell raiser. She had dumped him at the beginning of our senior year after he hit her one night when he was drinking.

I was in the Distributive Education Club, editor of the newspaper, and worked part time at a motel in Thomasville owned by Indians, which is where I got a good reference and first formed my philosophy of customer service, mainly stemming from my observation of what was done wrong. Jaden began dating me shortly thereafter and we'd been together, and happy, ever since. We had never discussed the incident of her being hit by Billy Ray, and in fact, most incidents crossing the social lines were quickly buried and never mentioned again, but everyone seemed to remember and used them as ammunition when needed. I'd heard Jaden's daddy had talked with Billy Ray's daddy and I may never know the outcome.

The rest of the ride was silent, and when we arrived, I stood back a while and watched people spilling from cars into the cemetery. Women's high heels sunk a bit into clay, making it an effort to get to the gravesite. Men reached down, grabbed weeds, and chewed on them.

As we moved toward the tent, I read tombstones, and one read "Her feet don't hurt no more." I didn't recall that one from childhood, but it struck me as odd someone would put that on a tombstone. We took our appointed seats underneath the green funeral tent with a few other relatives and friends, and the minister talked briefly and prayed. Once his Bible was closed, folks lined up, shook hands, and showed their respects to family members on the front row. After a few more handshakes and hugs, we made our way back to the car.

Back at Aunt Catfish's house, folks had brought food, while the house sitter prepared everything. A relatively new phenomenon, the house sitter was typically one of the people from the church who would come and make sure no one broke in and stole things while people were at a funeral. Criminals would read obituaries in the newspaper, then rob mourning family members. Once the Pavo Baptists had learned this, they set their plan of action in place, and though it had worked, there had never been a robbery prior to this new system. However, there were several stories circulating in town about mysterious cars that would slowly drive by to stake-out a house. No one could ever seem to get license plate numbers or a description because the windows had always been tinted.

Friends and family gathered and ate and talked into the early evening when Mama began doling out parcels of food for relatives to take home and eat again. Some of them didn't need to eat again, and I've never been to a funeral in Georgia where diet anything was served, but they would talk of diets and phrases such as "I'm going on a diet tomorrow," "I tried that one, but it didn't work and I'm gonna try another," or "The doctor says he can give me a prescription." If I'd learned anything from my parents and Catfish about the body, it was watching what you eat, eating normal portions, and getting regular exercise.

One of my only thin, and in fact, emaciated cousins, Doug, sat in a straight back chair. His eyes were glazed, and I figured he was high as a kite on marijuana or drunk or both. I hadn't seen him in two or three years and would probably never see him again, unless he felt he needed something from me, like borrow money that would never be repaid to support his habits. Catfish had been the glue of the family, and once the glue is gone, families crumble like stale bread. I knew I shouldn't have wondered, but I figured Doug would be the next funeral, and at his funeral no one would say, "Doug was a drug addict," "Doug was white trash," or "Doug will go to hell." Southerners, and more importantly Christians, are always striving to be nice and when Doug is dead, they will say, "Bless his heart, he had a hard life. I believe he was trying."

Doug's mama, Aunt Dorine had brought her newest, and fifth husband over after the service to meet everyone. "Max, honey, this is my husband, Frank. He delivers the potato chips to the grocery stores, and he can get you some free ones to take back to Tennessee."

"Nice to meet you, Frank." I shook his hand firmly, and it struck me odd that Dorine could now get free potato chips. Her fourth husband had been the Coke man and she ballooned up after she married him. I'd never met her third husband, since she was living on an alligator farm in Florida, but her second husband had been a trucker, and her first husband ran a doughnut shop in Tallahassee. She came home one day and caught him in bed with another woman and ran both of them in the street, naked, holding a gun on them until the police had coaxed her into putting the weapon down.

"I've never been to Nashville," said Frank.

"Well, you are both welcome to come see Jaden and me at any time," I lied, but it didn't matter. I knew they never would.

"Lord, it's getting late, Frank," said Dorine. "You've got to get up early for your route." They turned to go and part of me felt sorry for them. The years had passed for both, and they were still yearning for a happiness they had yet to find. Jaden calls me a pessimist, but I prefer realist because I know most people don't really want to change. Most want their cake and eat it, too. The ones who do change, do so from hard work and determination.

Once hugs were given and goodbyes were said, Mama, Daddy, and I sat on the front porch of Aunt Catfish's house. I sat in the swing, one of my favorite places on earth, and year after year, I told Jaden I wanted to buy one. I never had, and I guess it's because it wouldn't be Aunt Catfish's swing and probably because it would have to be a self-supporting, small swing to fit on our balcony overlooking the Cumberland River in Nashville. We settled for rocking chairs from Cracker Barrel instead.

Late afternoons, Aunt Catfish and I sat, swinging back and forth, not saying a word, and I would watch cars on Highway 122 going by. I would wonder where they were going and if life were more exciting once they got there. Somehow, I imagined it would be, and many times I had fallen asleep, being rocked and sung to by the metal chain squeaking against the hook in the ceiling, dreaming of change.

Chapter
2

Daddy swatted a mosquito on his leg and stood from one of the front porch rocking chairs he was in and told Mama it was time to go.

"Max, you gonna stay over here tonight, or you wanna come to the house?"

"I guess I'll just stay here, if ya'll don't mind. I need to do some work on my laptop and call Jaden. I'll probably stay a couple of days, since I have the time to take. I need to run over to Jaden's mama and daddy's before I go back and get some peaches to take back home."

Daddy said, "We'll be home, so just come on by anytime. Your mama fixed you a plate of leftovers in case you get hungry tonight or tomorrow, but your Aunt Ophelia probably had some food in there even though she didn't eat much. Why don't you go ahead and go through some of her stuff, if you have time, to see if there's anything you want to keep?"

"Okay, thanks," I said. I hugged them both goodbye, and as they walked across the yard, I noticed they had slowed, either by age or from exhaustion of the funeral. My guess would be the former. I stayed a little longer in the swing, watching fireflies until it got dark before going in and latching the screen door behind me. In the hallway, I flipped the switch to turn on the attic fan, and a cool breeze blew through the windows and through the screened door. Even though the temperature was already in the nineties in South Georgia, the Live Oak trees around the house kept some of the heat off.

Before it got too late, I thought I better call Jaden. If she'd had a rough day at school, she would want to take a bubble bath and go to bed early.

"Hey," I said.

"Hey. I'm glad you called. How was the service?

"Depressing."

"Max, I'm really sorry about your great aunt Ophelia, but it was time."

"It was past time," I said. "I'm not depressed about her passing. I just thought the service then the gathering over here at her house, was depressing."

"What was so depressing? It should have been a celebration."

"Well, first of all, she didn't look right. She didn't have a neck."

"You mean they had an open casket?"

"Yeah, but she wasn't banged up from the wreck or anything. It was the way they laid her in the casket that scrunched her neck up or something. I don't know. Then, all the relatives were over here. Doug was high or drunk as usual. Dorine was here with her fifth husband, a potato chip man, who can get us free chips, if you want."

"That's okay, but I do want you to go by Mama and Daddy's and get some peaches. See if Mama has any peaches she's put up. I wouldn't mind having some for a pie for the last day of school when we have our covered dish luncheon."

"I will. You tired?"

"Yeah, I'm going to take a bath and go to bed."

"Everything all right?"

"Yeah, there was a gun on campus today, so Metro had police everywhere, but it turned out to be a cap gun. I think the administration will still suspend the kid since they have a zero tolerance policy, but he's a good kid and he knew better."

"Yeah, he shouldn't push the limit. Well, I'll let you go. I love you."

"I love you, too. What's that loud humming noise?"

"Oh, that's the attic fan. I'm staying at Aunt Ophelia's."

"That's the first time I think I've ever heard you use her real name. Don't you think it's just a little creepy to stay over there?"

"I decided to quit calling her catfish now that she's gone, and no, I practically grew up in this house. Plus, Daddy wants me to go through some of the stuff and see if I want anything. You know, they've hinted at us coming back and living here, taking over this farm."

"Hmmm."

"What does that mean?"

"Well, that's something to think about."

"You mean you'd be interested in that?"

"Maybe. What in the world would you do?"

"I have no idea. If we did, would you teach?"

"Sure, I wouldn't want to give it up. I love teaching."

"Even though Billy Ray is the principal?"

"Max, that doesn't worry me one bit, but it must worry you."

"No, not really," I lied. "But, what about kids?"

"Okay, it's my bath time now. Call me tomorrow. Love you."

"Okay, love you, too. Sooner or later we really need to have this conversation."

"Yeah. Say hello to everyone."

"Okay, bye," I said, and the phone went dead. Jaden didn't have many traits that annoyed me, but not saying goodbye on the phone and just hanging up did annoy me. Her parents did the same thing, though, so I guess it was a learned behavior.

I wondered why Jaden didn't want to discuss having children. I figured being pregnant, and fat, probably bothered her more than anything, but I thought it would be fun to have a child. We would go shopping at Opry Mills in Nashville or the mall at Greenhill's and both of us marveled at the kids, sometimes stopping to tell them how cute they were, and I never understood why parents seemed so leery about that. They would look at us as if we were some suspicious child abductors or as if we had some kind of deformity that make people back up a little.

I walked around the house, looking at furniture. There were some nice antique pieces Jaden and I could probably use in our condo—a Queen Anne dining room suite, waterfall bedroom suite, an Ethan Allen chaise lounge that needed re-covering. I made a mental note to ask Daddy how serious he was about me taking stuff.

I walked in the kitchen, poured the last of a two-liter diet drink Mama had brought, which was already getting flat, and walked up the stairs. I thought if I could figure out how to keep drinks from becoming flat so soon after opening, I could probably sell the idea and make millions. I didn't feel comfortable sleeping in Aunt Ophelia's bed, so I went to the spare bedroom and opened my laptop. After logging into the exchange server for the hotel company site and checking my email, mostly junk the tech department couldn't keep out no more than postal workers could keep junk from being delivered, I looked in the closet and under the bed. In the back of the closet, partly hidden by boxes, I noticed a trunk and pulled it out. In it were letters addressed to Ophelia Peacock ranging from the 1920's to the 1950's from long gone family members and from other people I didn't recognize.

I vowed to read them all, but one dated 1941, with a three cent stamp, was from my great grandmother to Aunt Ophelia. I felt like a voyeur, but I couldn't resist.

Tues, a.m.
Dear Ophelia,
   This letter conveys a sad necessary to your brother as well as to you. I'm sure you have heard something about this condition and the trouble we have had, and know that Helen is now in the state hospital at Milledgeville. While we have been in Tallahassee visiting Aunt Mamie and Uncle Duncan, your sister Helen went all to pieces and they carried her to the hospital at Chattahoochee where she stayed two days until they could secure transportation for her to go to Milledge-

ville. I wanted to ask if you and your brother might be able to go see her as we just aren't able to make the trip and hope to be back home at Tallokas soon. My gout is bothering me and your daddy has a bad cough. I'm afraid he might have to go to a doctor here. Helen wrote me that she tried to get home, but just couldn't. To make a long story short, we just had to send her away for treatment. Everyone says the State Hospital is the best place for her, and the doctor writes that she is fairly well. I can see now that she has not been herself for more than a year, even when we were at home, but we just didn't know what was wrong. Pray for Helen. I'm afraid she won't be home for a while. I fear she has what your father's mother had, and you know she never recovered. I wish you and Jack well and hope to see you by Christmas. God bless you both.
*   Lovingly,*
*   Mother*

I didn't know what to think. Not only did I not know that my great aunt Helen had been admitted to a state mental hospital, but I didn't know I had a great aunt Helen. Aunt Ophelia had certainly never mentioned a Helen, and my daddy had never mentioned anything about an Aunt Helen that I recalled either. Of course, Grandfather Peacock had died young from a heart attack, and I never knew him, but Granny Peacock never made mention of an Aunt Helen.

When the phone rang, it startled me. I wasn't expecting a call, but figured it was Jaden calling me back.

"Hello?"

"Max, honey, I've got some news. Your cousin, Doug, has been put in the detox unit in Thomasville. Dorine called just a little while ago and said Doug came home and just flipped. Took a gun and began shooting up the house. Dorine said he was going through withdrawals."

"Mama, earlier when he was over here, he looked high or drunk."

"No, he wasn't. He was sick. Dorine said he hadn't had

nothing in a few days. Said he was trying to quit, bless his heart. He's had a hard life."

Just as I figured. "Well, why in the world was he shooting up the house?"

"Dorine said he was seeing a little man who was pointing and laughing at him. Said he finally got a gun and chased the little man through the house. Wherever the little man went and stood, he took a shot. Said he went and got in the refrigerator and Doug shot up the refrigerator. The little man went and got on the sofa and he shot up the sofa. He'd already shot a hole in his closet door where the little man was hiding. Finally, the little man went outside and climbed a tree and Doug kept shooting in the tree. Once Doug was out the door, Dorine and Frank locked him out and called the law. It took them a while to get there, and I'm sure they didn't want to go, but they chained his ankles and cuffed his hands and took him to detox. At least they'll give him some medication to bring him back to his senses, but maybe he's learned his lesson. Dorine thought you might want to go visit him and talk to him. She said he always looked up to you. Maybe you can help him."

"That's awful. You reckon he was seeing a leprechaun?"

"Max, that ain't funny."

"You're right, but I'm not a counselor. I'll go see him, but I can't help him. He's got to help himself."

"Well, that's true, but you could try. Ain't no harm in trying."

"Okay, I'll go over there tomorrow. Listen, who was Aunt Helen?"

"Why in the world are you asking about her?"

"I found some letters in a trunk in the spare room and saw one from Great Grandma Peacock to Aunt Ophelia. I know I shouldn't have read them, but Daddy told me to go through her things to see if there was anything I wanted."

"He wasn't talking about personal things. Your daddy would have a fit if he knew you'd found out about his daddy's sister."

"Well, what happened to her? Is she still in Milledge-ville?"

"Lord, no, she's been dead for years. She lost her mind. They had to do a procedure on her. You'll have to ask your daddy." She paused and yelled, "Jack, come here and talk to Max."

Dad picked up the phone and asked, "Max, something wrong?"

"No, not really."

"Why'd you call then?"

"I didn't call. Mama called me to tell me about Doug."

"What happened to Doug?"

"She'll tell you about that. What I want to know is who is Helen?"

"Helen was my aunt, my daddy's sister. How'd you hear about Helen?"

"Well, I found a trunk and was looking through some of its contents and found a letter."

"Son, I don't think you need to be worrying yourself about such things. Helen's been dead for years. Probably thirty or forty years."

"What happened to her?"

"I don't know. She had some condition. They had to put her in Milledgeville and she died in Milledgeville. She wouldn't have been able to come home. My daddy, mama, and even Ophelia never really talked about it much."

"Did anyone look into it?"

"Look into what?"

"Look into what killed her?"

"I don't know. They did a procedure on her forehead, and she lived on, but she was more like a vegetable. She could get around, but she really didn't know much after that."

"They call that a prefrontal lobotomy. Good God, I can't believe it."

"Why are you worrying about that?"

"I don't know. I guess because if Jaden and I had kids, something could be genetic. In the letter, Great Grandma said Great Grandpa's mama had it, too. What was it they had?"

"I don't know enough about it to know what they would call it today. They mainly just acted crazy. Back then we just didn't talk about stuff like that."

"Well, how'd they act crazy? What did they say?"

"I don't know. They just weren't right. Talked to things. Saw things that weren't there. Always thought the government was after them."

"That is odd."

"Yeah, it's odd, but you don't need to worry about that."

"Well, thanks, Dad. I'll see ya'll tomorrow."

"Okay, why don't you come eat some lunch with us? Your mama's gonna cook some fried green tomatoes and I've just finished boiling some peanuts."

"Sounds good to me."

I wanted to call Jaden, but knew she'd be trying to sleep and didn't want to bother her. Unlike Jaden, I never had problems falling asleep. She would occasionally get insomnia, which her mother also had, but I would lie down on the bed, on a sofa, in a doctor's office, or where ever, and I would be out. The last thing I remembered was lying down in bed, and I was startled when I awoke from the screams of the peacocks Aunt Ophelia kept and fed in the adjacent woods.

Still dressed from the night before, I went downstairs and made coffee. The house was cool from the breeze the attic fan had pulled in all night, and in the morning air, there was a faint smell of honeysuckle. I put on a pot of coffee, went to the restroom, poured a cup and sat outside on the porch. No wonder people could live into the nineties here, I mused. Everything was still. Contrary to Nashville, where there was always something happening and traffic galore with three major interstates coming through downtown, Pavo was still and peaceful. Even though our condo was on the Cumberland River and we had a balcony, it wasn't as peaceful. There were barges and tugboats early in the morning, and the smog from the city made one not really want to sit outside all the time. The birds, too, were different. Sure, there were Thrashers, Cardinals, Blue Jays, Crows, etc., but I would see bluebirds in Tennessee and couldn't recall when I'd seen one in Georgia. Too, there were coastal scavenger birds in Nashville that I only recall seeing at the beach as a child. It seemed

to me they had moved inland for the garbage they had become accustomed to in highly developed coastal areas.

Gulping the last of my coffee, I walked back inside Aunt
Ophelia's house. If she were here, I would have a big breakfast. She, along with my parents, believed in eating a big
breakfast with scrambled eggs, bacon, and toast. I generally
had a breakfast bar and coffee unless I went to Cracker Barrel, which I imagined was successful, in part, because of their
ability to tap into those collective memories, and this is illus-
trated in their décor as well.

I took a quick shower, poured another cup of coffee,
logged on to my laptop to delete junk email, and readied myself for the day. I knew I would drive over to the hospital and
see Doug and try to be back at my parents' house in Pavo for
lunch. My cell rang and it was Jaden.

"Good morning. How'd you sleep?" she asked.

"Great," I said. "How about you?"

"You know I didn't sleep well. I can't sleep as well if
you're not here. All the more reason for you to come on
home."

"Jaden, I'm going to stay until Sunday. I'm going over
to the hospital to see Doug this morning. He was admitted to
the detox unit last night after hallucinating and shooting up
the house."

"Oh, my God. Was anyone hurt?"

"I don't think so."

"Why was he hallucinating? You said he was on something after the funeral."

"No, according to Mama, he was drying out and began
hallucinating. He kept seeing a little man, like a leprechaun,
who was pointing and laughing at him. Then, he decided to
shoot the little man and chased him all over the house firing a
shotgun. Finally, he went outside and was shooting at the little man when Aunt Dorine called the law."

"A little man like a leprechaun?"

"I don't know. Sounds crazy, but I've heard of people
seeing little people before."

"Yeah? What were they on?"

"Nothing. I don't know what the significance of that would be."

"None, I'm sure."

"Anyway, after I see Doug, I'll go eat lunch with my parents. I don't have any other plans. It kind of bothers me that I don't."

"Lord, Max, just chill. Enjoy your day. Do what you want. You don't always have to have a plan." Jaden was right. I typically became anxious when I didn't have something to do. I just couldn't sit still.

"Okay, I will. Listen, I want to tell you something. I found an old letter I read in a trunk upstairs last night. It was from my great grandmother Peacock to Aunt Ophelia and my granddaddy. They had a sister named Helen who was put in Milledgeville for some mental disorder. She must have had a lobotomy in there, and at some point, she died. Is that wild or what?"

"Oh, dear Heavens. I've never heard you mention an Aunt Helen. Don't recall anyone ever mentioning her either."

"Me neither, which is what makes it so odd. You know how people around here talk."

"Yeah, and I don't recall my parents saying anything about a Helen."

"I'm a little curious if I can get some more information. You know, from a genetic perspective, we need to know these things, if we have children."

"Well, I'm running late. Traffic will be bad this morning because of the fog from the river. I'll call you when I get home. I can't believe your phone picks up out there."

"Yeah, me, too. Hope you have a good day."

"Thanks. Love you." She was gone.

After I put on my jeans, tennis shoes, and a polo shirt, I headed to my Jeep Cherokee. I almost didn't lock the door because I knew I would come back at some point during the day, but then I remembered the funeral sitter and turned around to go back and lock up the house. I always locked doors in Nashville, however, and in fact, I would usually check and recheck to make sure I had.

Chapter
<u>3</u>

I turned the air conditioning on and scanned for radio channels, finding nothing but the religious station of South Georgia—W.A.F.T.—which, interestingly enough, comes from the hymn "Jesus Saves" and was the sign-on and sign-off for the station with a choir singing, "Waft it on the rolling tide, Jesus saves, Jesus saves." At any given time, one could hear either instrumental or old-time gospel music, preaching by a variety of protestant ministers who huff and puff, and advertising of events held at area churches—bingo at the Presbyterian church, a Lottie Moon supper at the Baptist church, a special healing service for soldiers at the Pentecostal church, a Bible study on the end of time at the holiness church, where it seemed they used fear of hell to get people to believe.

For whatever reason, I wasn't in the mood and popped in a Fleetwood Mac CD and turned it up for the twenty-minute drive to the detox unit in Thomasville. I mused that if the townspeople of Pavo heard me listening to Stevie Nicks on the way to Thomasville, they would begin rumors I was a warlock or devil worshipper, but some people just don't like good music. Plus, not everyone who lives in Nashville listens to country music all the time.

As I stopped at the one traffic light, the city policeman, a guy we called Buddy and who I graduated high school with, nodded, his eyes unscrutable behind the reflective sunglasses. The last time I had seen Buddy, he had put on forty pounds, and had three children by his current wife. He had been quite the stud in high school—the guy with the brand new spiffy truck, the brand name clothes, and the I-don't-care attitude that drove the girls nuts, since high school girls thrive on emotions, whether good or bad.

Buddy and I had been friends in elementary school, where on the playground I had once dared him to pick up and bite a crusty dog turd for five dollars. He did and got mad because I didn't have five dollars. We were friends in junior high school, too, but in high school, we drifted apart for whatever reason. It could have been because I turned into a barfly, hopping from bars in Tallahassee to Valdosta, drinking hardcore liquor, and grew my hair over my ears, a signal to family something was wrong. I had even been banned from one bar in Valdosta at seventeen—though the drinking age was eighteen, one could easily get alcohol—for dirty dancing on the table with my girlfriend, Sandi, who had been my girlfriend in my junior year. Sandi ended up in detox a few years later before marrying an Air Force jet technician and moving to a Texas Air Force base.

Stevie Nicks was singing "Gold Dust Woman," and I felt a sense of power at the beat of the music and a sense of completeness at the lyrics. Buddy had stayed country, wearing rattlesnake skin boots and belts, drinking beer, and doing silly things on weekend nights like cow tipping. None of these phases lasted, of course, when the reality of graduation hit and teens got jobs, go into the military, or go to college. Buddy had gone to the police academy, and I had gone to college. Right before college and after Jaden and I became a couple our senior year, I had cut my black locks of hair and straightened up. Instead of drinking hardcore liquor, Jaden and I explored wine, and even today, we visit wineries and give wine at Christmas when we come home to Georgia. Aunt Ophelia loved wine and believed a glass a day increased longevity.

As I left Pavo for Thomasville, I was overwhelmed by

the pecan orchards, pine tree forests, and the live oak trees draped in Spanish moss, creating canopy roads that are cool during the day, but eerie at night. As odd as it may be for someone who wasn't an arborist, there's something about the landscape of where one is born and raised that becomes a part of him.

One log truck after another passed, and it occurred to me that I didn't know what happened to the logger who hit Aunt Ophelia. I wondered if he was on the road hauling logs in Thomas County, and reflected on if he had any remorse. I realized it was different than a drunk driver who might kill someone in a head-on collision, but I believed one would have to feel something for someone dying from any accident they caused.

Even before Doug became hooked on alcohol and drugs, he was hit head-on by a group of girls out joyriding. They had crossed the center line, not paying attention because they were singing, and smashed into his Camaro, causing both cars to spin, theirs winding up in a ditch. Coming to his senses, Doug had jumped out and ran to the driver's side, where he held the girl's hand as she spit blood and faded in and out of consciousness. Through no fault of his own, Doug was affected by the accident. He attended the all black funeral, hearing whispers, getting stares, and even being the recipient of some reverse racial comments. I wondered if somehow the accident hadn't been the impetus for his spiritual downfall.

I passed a white clapboard siding house. Egg cartons were cut out and stuck on the limbs of a bush. Tires were painted white and planted in the ground at the driveway keeping drivers from running into the ditch. An old washing machine and sofa rested on the porch. Lawn chairs sat around a tree to the side of the house while older cars with sparkling new wheels parked haphazardly in the dirt yard. It seemed odd someone would spend several hundred dollars on new wheels for an old car.

Several family members stood talking and all waved and I waved back, a behavior that is tradition among all people in the rural South. I had to wonder if the greeting was authentic or based on some conditioned response. To me, it was a depressing scene, seeing people live beneath the poverty level and living from one government check to the next. In the rural South where farming had declined, where manufacturing jobs had gone to Mexico or China to begin a new era of slavery disguised as free trade, and where anyone with the least amount of perception could have seen the lone political wolf Perot was right about the giant sucking sound, I had wanted to leave and move to a big city, where life seemed to be more thriving and where Jaden and I could have a successful life.

As I slowed my Cherokee and turned down the music, I drove through the historical district of Thomasville. Beautiful historical homes, rumored to be haunted, lined the streets of downtown and turning onto Main Street, the Jeep vibrated as the tires rolled across the brick street. Just past Main Street, the three hundred year old majestic oak stood as a reminder of nature's endurance with its twenty-four feet circumference. The resurrection fern growing on its one hundred sixty-two limb spread created an awesome ambiance that had even impressed President Eisenhower when he'd once visited.

Turning onto Country Club Drive, I thought a state mental hospital in this area was somehow ironic, and as I weaved the Cherokee down the long driveway, I was fortunate to have found a parking space at the front entrance, even though all of the handicap spaces were vacant. Somehow, I was always irritated with the vast emptiness of handicap spaces in front of businesses, but what irritated me more, was seeing people park, hang their handicap tags that they don't hang until needed, and get out and run into a business. The only handicap I thought they probably had was a lazy handicap.

When I entered the stark building, the receptionist was kind, and as she walked around the desk to show me where Doug's room was located, I wanted to tell her to pull her pants out of her butt crack. I don't know why I had always been a butt man, but I had always been fascinated with them. Jaden's butt was the first thing which attracted me to her, but I'd never told her that. What was more fascinating to me about butts was how people could let their underwear, and even pants, creep in there and not notice, not to mention the whole concept of a thong, which I found disgusting, worn by women who should have taken their mothers' advice about wearing clean underwear just a step further to include not wearing a thong that crawled into places it shouldn't be going into in the first place.

Taking her pointing as a cue and walking further down the hallway, I could hear moans and groans coming from different rooms. I found Doug's room, cracked the door, and peered inside. Doug seemed asleep, his arms and legs strapped to the bed. His sandy blonde hair stuck out everywhere and his face revealed beard stubble. He heard the door.

"Who's there?"

"Doug, it's me. Max. You awake?"

"Yeah, Max, come in."

"How're you feeling?"

"I've seen better days, but I've seen the light."

"What do you mean?"

"I went down a tunnel, saw a light. Aunt Ophelia was there holding out her arms to me like I was still a child and cut myself or something. I wanted to go on into the light, but something was pulling me back. I know now that I was in the presence of God and he's spared me."

I had read of near death experiences, but generally, I thought they were associated with heart attacks, not withdrawals, but I believed if it helped Doug quit all those drugs and alcohol, then it would be fine. "I'm just glad you're all right."

"I told the nurse in the night when it happened and asked her to call Reverend Mason to come see me. I feel I've had an instant change. It's like a peace, a warmth, came over me, and I know I won't drink or do drugs again. I know I have a purpose and mission now. I should get out in a day or two. When're you leaving for Tennessee?"

"I guess I'll leave in a few days. I'm not sure just yet."

"Will you go to church with me Sunday, Max?"

"Well, I don't know if I'll still be here."

"If you are, will you go? Some of the best memories I have

when we were kids is going to church with Aunt Ophelia."

"Yeah, me too. If I'm still here on Sunday, I'll go. Be nice to go there without it being a funeral."

"Thanks." Doug seemed tired and nodded, his eyelids almost closing and then reopening briefly. It was clear to me he needed to rest.

"Sure. I guess I better go and let you rest. I need to get back to Mama and Daddy's house for lunch."

"Okay, Max."

"Listen, if you need anything, call. I can bring you some clothes or something if you want."

"No, that's okay. Mama will come later on today and bring me stuff. I think if they can just take me out of these straps, I'll be more comfortable."

I hated seeing Doug strapped in the bed like that. If he had an itch, he couldn't even scratch. "You want me to ask them to undo the straps?" I'm not sure I would have if he responded "yes," but I wanted to.

"They will in a while. It's protocol to prevent people from hurting themselves. I might've yesterday, but today, I won't hurt myself ever again."

I hoped he was right. "Okay, I'll see you."

"See you."

I walked back down the hall, went outside and was hit with the humidity, got in my Jeep, and took the side and back roads to the highway to head back to Pavo. I somehow felt that Doug would be all right. At least I hoped so. Part of me believed his problem was genetic from his daddy's side of the family—a whole bunch of alcoholics. I recalled my mother's mother, Granny Finny, telling me about her granddaddy, my great-great granddaddy, who liked to partake. When they would hear him coming down the lane in the buggy, they could hear the cracking of the whip and him cursing and shooting his pistol, and they would all hide in the woods until he passed out. Then they'd be called home by whoever was still awake and sleep half a day the next day, only waking to doctor bug bites. Finally, he ran off with a fourteen year-old girl, had children with her, and then married the girl's mama.

It wasn't something the family talked about much, and it's a wonder I hadn't inherited that from my mama's side of the family. I figured had I not stopped drinking hard liquor when I was young, I might have turned out a bit like him. Of course, Doug and I partied together a lot in high school before I quit drinking so much. Doug had been the daredevil. We'd skip school, go to the river, and Doug would drive his truck so fast across sand dunes, we'd be in the air before we'd land on the next dune. I had not wanted him to do it, for fear we'd be hurt, or worse yet, killed, and I had vowed to get him back.

Once when we were in a country bar in Valdosta, I got an older woman named Ethel to dance with him. Ethel practically lived there. Sometimes she had her teeth in and sometimes she didn't, but she'd get drunk and stay on the dance floor all night, whether by herself or not. I told Ethel it was Doug's birthday, and he wanted to dance with her since she was the best dancer in the bar. Then like a periscope on a submarine, Ethel focused her sight on Doug, pulled him to the dance floor, and they fast danced. When the slow song began, she pulled him close, and about half-way through, her hands slipped to his butt cheeks and she grabbed hold. Doug's eyes opened wide and his face turned red as a tomato. Everyone at our table laughed, and I laughed so hard I gagged. It took some time for Doug to speak to me again and forgive me for my practical joke. He said he'd get me back, but if he did, I didn't know about it.

There was another part of me, however, who felt Doug's issues had been caused by his mama marrying so many different men and him having to call them all daddy, which I always thought was odd. I honestly didn't understand Aunt Dorine's need to keep getting married. I always felt she was stuck between generations. One generation was my grandmother's. These women were strong and ran a household and all that went along with it, even if it meant suffering themselves. The new generation felt the need to work and be more independent, and tried to do both. Aunt Dorine was less independent, and I believe if she'd become educated, she could have accomplished much more. But it seemed to be much easier to do nothing and blame mistakes on others instead of oneself.

Personally, I considered myself fortunate to have had both parents all my life, not that they always got along or agreed, but they never let the petty stuff get in the way of their life together.

Once when my daddy joined a pyramid scheme some of the other deacons at the Baptist church had conned him into joining, he'd drawn out savings and didn't tell Mama. When she got something in the mail and started asking questions, he'd turned red and confessed. She threw him out of the house, and he went to Aunt Ophelia's house for about a week until he apologized and promised to put more money back in savings.

I remember she'd be cooking in the kitchen, and I'd be watching television in the den, and she'd just yell out of no-where, "Gambling is no better than drinking."

I figured if he would have somehow struck it rich, she wouldn't have been so mad, but he didn't. None of the deacons had, actually, and a couple of them lost their houses, but the church supported them until they could get back on their feet.

By the time I got to Mama and Daddy's house in Pavo, they were a little antsy, since they typically eat lunch at ten in the morning because they get up at four a.m. I figured their blood sugar levels were low and that problem presents itself as antsy.

"Where you been?" Mama asked.

"I visited with Doug for a little while and then came straight back."

"You must've slept late,"

"I don't remember what time it was."

"Well, just because you are off don't mean you can sleep all day."

"Sorry," I said. I didn't know what else to say.

"How's Doug doin' this morning?" she asked.

"I think he'll be all right. He had a conversion experi-ence."

"What do you mean?"

"Well, he said he went in a tunnel to the light, saw Aunt Ophelia, and felt the presence of God. Said he won't touch another drop or do any more drugs. Said he's gonna go to church Sunday and wanted me to go with him."

"Praise God," said Mama. "What church is he gonna go to?"

"I assume the Baptist church because he had the nurses call Reverend Mason for him about the vision."

"I know what the sermon will be about then, if he told him what he'd seen. I knew that boy would come around to his senses sooner or later. Now if we could just get Dorine back in church, but with all those husbands she's had, I don't know what people would think about that."

"They wouldn't think nothing," said Daddy. Daddy always got defensive about his sister, Dorine. He glared at me. "Well, don't just stand there lookin' like a deer in the headlights, get yourself a plate."

I put fresh beans, ham and fried green tomatoes on my plastic plate, poured a glass of sweetened iced tea and sat down to eat. Daddy said a quick prayer, the long ones being reserved for major family gatherings, and I dug in. I didn't realize how hungry I was.

"Don't forget I got some boiled peanuts, Max," Daddy said.

"I'll have to take some for later tonight."

"Have you thought any more about moving back? Taking over your Aunt Ophelia's house?"

"Not really. Just haven't had time yet to give it much thought." My parents became animated for some reason, and I assumed it was because I was there. Normally, there wasn't this much conversation, choosing instead not to talk and watching the wallpaper peel off the wall.

"You really ought to. You could rent out your condo in Nashville, Jaden could get a job in the school system here, and you could convert your Aunt Ophelia's house into a bed and breakfast." Daddy seemed excited about his ideas, and quite frankly, he had excited me somewhat because I had not thought of the bed and breakfast idea. Aunt Ophelia's house would make a good bed and breakfast.

"That's a good idea, but I don't know that we'd have the occupancy rate to break even."

"Well, you've got historical Thomasville, the Agricultural Expo in Moultrie, the Mayhaw Festival, the Creek Indian Festival, the Fire Ant Festival in Ashburn, not to mention the Pavo Festival and other tourist draws. Plus, businessmen would rather stay there than stay in a chain, since their companies will pay higher prices anyway. I'd say it would work. You could also incorporate, call the Peacock place a hunting plantation, and do guided tours. That's pretty big in Thomas County now. Even the Secretary of Defense came down and hunted here a few months back."

"Those are good ideas. You're certainly making a good case. I'll talk to Jaden about it. I think she'd be open to it. She does want to help take care of her parents when they get older."

"That's nice," said Mama. "It's the way it ought to be, but now-a-days, they just throw you in a nursing home and wait for you to die. And them nursing homes ain't nothing to write home about either. A lot of them just want the money. And if you've seen them TV shows, a lot of them abuse the people. Somebody ought to do something about that. It's just a shame. I don't ever want to be put in a nursing home."

Daddy and I nodded. "These fried green tomatoes are great, Mama," I said. "I don't know when I've had some of these. You just can't get them in Tennessee. You can't get boiled peanuts either. In fact, most people don't eat them in Tennessee. I made some one night when we had neighbors over for a Titans game. They all thought it was sick that someone would eat wet, salted peanuts. I really couldn't believe it."

"That right there tells you something's wrong with them if they won't eat boiled peanuts," said Mama.

I laughed and told Mama she was probably right. Of course, most of the time she was right about everything. What did trouble me was that she prided herself in being right.

Chapter
4

After lunch, Mama, Daddy, and I went into the den. We were all full, and Daddy sat in the recliner and changed the channel to CNN Headline News. Mama sat in the other recliner and picked up the latest issue of *Country Living*. I stretched out on the sofa and toed my shoes off. I knew I needed to get over to Jaden's parents, but I felt tired.

"It's time for *The Young and the Restless*," Mama said.

"Max and I ain't gonna watch that," Daddy objected.

I wished Daddy had left me out of it. Nothing irritated me more than being pulled into the middle of a disagreement between them, except Jaden not saying goodbye when she hung up the phone.

"Well, I need to know what's gonna happen to Ms. Chancellor."

"You'll still be able to find out tomorrow," Daddy said. "They never tell you the whole thing in one show."

"How would you know?" Mama asked.

"I've tried to watch them before."

"When?"

"Long time ago."

Mama flipped the pages even louder and didn't say much for a while, and while the news anchor spouted head-lines, I closed my eyes. I didn't want to take a nap, but I was even more tired than I thought. In a few minutes Mama said, "Something's going on with that Freda woman."

"What?" Daddy asked.

"You heard me. You mark my word. That woman named Freda who joined the church a month ago after she shot her husband and got off claiming abuse is up to something."

"What do you think she's up to?" Daddy asked.

"I think she's after the preacher."

"Lord have mercy. Where'd you come up with that notion?"

"I'm telling you. You mark my word. I've noticed the way they look at each other."

At this point, I was sitting up on the sofa, eyes wide open. "Who in the world shot her husband and claimed abuse? Freda who?" Minor crimes happened all over the county, but it was truly a rarity there was a murder.

"Oh, you know them, Max. You went to school with one of their daughters. Don't recall her name, but their last name is Yates."

"Meghan Yates?"

"Yeah, that's her," Mama said. "They never did go to church anywhere that I know of, but they weren't from here originally. They were from Atlanta. They moved down here for Mr. Yates' job at the coat factory in Thomasville. Story goes he was mean to all of them. Said he would lock his wife in the dog pens at night and make her clean them with Clorox. Wouldn't let the woman out till they were clean. There's some who said the old man raped his daughters, too."

"I can't believe this. When did this happen? Why didn't you call me?"

"Well," Mama said. "Didn't seem to be that big of a deal that she joined the church. I would've told you if I thought about it."

"No," I said, "not that. I didn't know Mrs. Yates had killed her husband. Jaden and I would've sent Meghan and their family a card or something. I think Jaden was friends with her, and she was actually my girlfriend in elementary school. Don't you remember buying that heart-shaped box of candy on Valentine's Day and that red teddy bear from the Rexall drug store?"

"Lord, I can't hardly remember what day it is, let alone what happened thirty years ago. Plus, you always had one girlfriend or another," Mama said.

Daddy chimed in. "Yeah, the girls were always after you. What's the name of that one I liked? I figured ya'll would end up getting married."

"You liked her," Mama said. "Max didn't."

I couldn't recall which girl Daddy was talking about, but apparently she made an impression on him, and quite frankly, I wondered why they thought I had so many girlfriends because I did not, especially ones who were what I would call serious. "Was there a trial or something?"

"No," Mama said. "They had a hearing. Two of the daughters were so messed up they sent them off somewhere to live with some relatives. I think there was a son, too, but I don't know what happened to him. Freda held her head high, though. We all took food to her house, and I guess she was so taken with our kindness, she came to church about a month ago. When the church was on the fourth verse of "Just As I Am," she came marching down the aisle, rededicated her life, and joined the church. She was crying, and she and the preacher were hugging. Of course, everyone went up front to shake hands and welcome her, and everyone felt sorry for her and what she must've gone through. I couldn't even sleep, knowing she'd shot him in the privates then shot him in the head. I kept wondering how in the world she could stay in the house after that, but Freda must be strong, and getting stronger, because she's been in church every time the door is open. But I have noticed the way she and the preacher look at each other. Other people have noticed it, too, and Miss Emma said his car has been over at her house quite a bit."

"How does she know that?" Daddy asked.

"I guess she's seen it over there."

"She don't even live out that way. What's she doing, driving by and being nosy? So she can stir something up?"

"No," Mama said. "Emma was probably out just joy riding. She wouldn't drive by just to be nosy. She tells it like she sees it."

"The telling it is what concerns me," Daddy said. "Starting rumors will just cause a ruckus."

"Poor Mrs. Mason," said Mama, shaking her head back and forth. "Granted, she's a little homely, but that woman has a heart of gold and is a solid Christian, but when you put the two of them side by side, it's crystal clear Mrs. Yates looks better, even through all that caked-on make-up and all that dye in her hair. Still, it just ain't right."

"I trust the preacher. Remember, I was the head of the deacon committee who hired him."

"I know. But he's not Jesus. He's a man."

"I know that," Daddy said. "I trust the man. He's just trying to do the right thing and help her. I feel sure nothing is going on. He's one of the best preachers we've ever had."

"Nobody said he wasn't," Mama argued. "But a man's a man and something else might be thinking for him." Mama smiled, and I wondered with her look and his facial expression if this had somehow become personal.

I wondered if either had ever had an affair, and immediately on thinking it, I felt guilty. I couldn't imagine them sleeping together, let alone sleeping with someone else. Thinking of one's parents having sex isn't the best of thoughts, and I remember what Aunt Dorine had said about Granny Peacock at some point—that some widower she dated would spend the night.

That gave me chills, thinking my grandmother might be sleeping with someone, but the biggest shocker of all was when Aunt Dorine had said to me years earlier, "Max, you are so naïve. Why don't you ask your Granny how she likes marijuana?"

All these years later, and I still remember those words, echoing in my mind like the loudest alarm clock on earth. I knew Granny Peacock had sight problems and tried a number of medicinal cures, and maybe that's why she tried it.

Daddy's recliner bolted forward, and he got up and went

out in the garage to piddle. Mama, too, got up, walked over to his recliner, grabbed the remote, changed the channel to *The Young and the Restless*, looked at me as she was sitting back down in her recliner, and asked, "Max, you don't mind if I change it, do you?"

"No," I said. "We've seen the headlines, and now they're just repeats." I didn't mind at all, but I wondered if Mama hadn't brought all that up about the preacher because she knew it would upset Daddy, he would leave, and she would get to watch her TV show.

I stood and told Mama I needed to get over to Jaden's parents. She asked what I was doing for supper, and I told her I would either eat supper with Jaden's parents or just pick up a sandwich in town—that after the delicious lunch I was stuffed and couldn't eat much anyway.

"Well, call us later." Mama never took her eyes off the soap opera. I walked out into the garage.

"Max, I just don't believe that about the preacher. It would be awful if it were true."

"Yes, that wouldn't be good."

"I probably ought to call some of the other deacons and meet and discuss it. We'll have to confront him about it. If Miss Emma is telling it, everyone in town knows."

I chuckled. "She always was a little nosy, don't you think?"

"And apparently still is, even at her age, but she was the best alto the choir ever had."

"I think I'm gonna run over to Jaden's parents, pick up some stuff, and visit with them a while. Then I'll run back over to Aunt Ophelia's and try to work a little and make some calls."

"Okay. You want to come eat supper?"

"I told Mama I'd pass. I'm still full. I might eat with Jaden's parents."

"All right. We'll see you tomorrow then. Tell them hey."

"I will. I'll call ya'll later on this evening."

I got in the Cherokee and eased out of the driveway, looking in both directions, even though Oak Street wasn't as heavily traveled as Highway 122 by Aunt Ophelia's. I turned the air on high. It seemed even hotter in South Georgia than normal and humid, too. My t-shirt underneath my polo shirt felt soggy.

As I drove through town, Buddy was still parked in the same spot as he had been earlier in the day, and I wondered if his eyes were closed behind his reflective sunglasses. Part of me wanted to stop and say hello, but I felt pressed for time, and really didn't know what we'd talk about. I drove on through town and turned off on Egg and Butter Road, which I always thought was the strangest name for a clay road and conjured up, I imagine, by someone with high cholesterol who probably didn't know he had it.

The clay road was smooth and flanked the Okapilco Creek, a deep black water creek. In the murkier parts, where old Cypress stumps stood, mayhaw berries grew on trees along the muddy banks. I recalled Aunt Ophelia taking Doug and me to pick mayhaws when we were children, and neither of us liked the taste of the small red berry, but when Aunt Ophelia made the jelly, we ate it on biscuits every chance we got. We'd poke a finger through the center of the biscuit, dig around, and fill the hole with jelly. There wasn't anything else like that in the world. On very special occasions, she would treat us to a mayhaw jelly cake.

Thinking about those good times made me feel wispy. I rounded the corner and crossed the wooden bridge, where the Okapilco was deepest and where kids often swung from ropes fastened in a Live Oak and splashed into the murky water below. Jaden had done this quite a bit with friends who lived in this part of the county, but I had never done it for fear of water moccasins. Jaden had told me that all the noise the kids made scared the water moccasins off, but I had my doubts. Rounding a sharp curve in the clay road, I spotted the antique iron wagon wheel painted black with a mailbox welded onto the top part of the wheel at the edge of driveway. I turned in and followed the two-lane path lined with azaleas up to the circular drive in front of the Cape Cod.

When I stepped out of the Cherokee, I could smell the

peaches. Off to the side of the house was what Jaden called the peach shed, where people unloaded the peaches and put them in crates to ship. I'd noticed the workers had changed in the past ten years. At some point in time, all agriculture work was done by poor blacks and whites. Now, the blacks and whites had all but disappeared and the workers were Mexican. Even though I was stuffed, I still always felt hungry when I smelled the aroma of peaches.

Jaden's dad waved and walked toward the front of the house.

"Max, good to see you." He reached out a hand and I took it. His grip was solid.

"You, too."

"We were hoping we'd get to see you while you were here. I'm really sorry about your Great Aunt Ophelia. I wished we could have come to the service, but we had to get peaches shipped that day."

"Thanks. It was a nice service. I don't want to hold you up from work."

"No, that's okay. They know what to do. Come on in. Doris made some fresh lemonade this morning."

"Sounds good to me."

Ed and I walked up the brick steps, opened the painted red wooden door, and went inside. "Doris," yelled Ed. "Max is here."

I could hear Doris walking out of one of the bedrooms upstairs, the wooden floors creaking with each step. "Hey Max," she greeted, descending the stairs.

"Hey. You doing all right?"

"I sure am, but I'd be doing better if I had a grandbaby." She hugged me and Ed chuckled.

"What would you do if they had a child, Doris? You wouldn't stay in the big city of Nashville for too long."

"Yeah, but I keep hoping and praying Jaden and Max will move home."

"They won't ever move back," Ed snorted. "Once you have a taste of big city life, you can't go back. Ain't that right, Max?"

"I don't know. We've talked about moving back one of these days. Daddy wants me to take over Aunt Ophelia's place."

"Oh, I knew it!" Doris grabbed me and hugged me again. "And I just know my prayers about a grandbaby will come true."

"Well," I said. "We have discussed having children."

"Praise the Lord," Doris said.

"Doris, that don't mean they're gonna have one anytime soon," Ed said.

"They will. Talking about it is a sign they're ready."

"I'm ready, but I'm not sure Jaden is."

"Oh, she is. She just has doubts, but she'll come around."

"Maybe, but I'm a little worried about genetics."

"Genetics?" Doris asked.

"Yeah, apparently there's a history of mental illness in Daddy's line. Aunt Ophelia had a sister who died in Milledgeville. Daddy doesn't know what was wrong with her, and I think it even went back another generation."

"Oh, don't worry about that kind of stuff. Things are different now," Doris said. "Come on, let's go in the kitchen. I just made some fresh lemonade."

We all walked into the kitchen. The kitchen always smelled like garlic because of the cloves hanging. There was also a bin that was never without fresh vegetables. I knew Jaden had grown up eating healthy and couldn't hardly have a meal without a salad. The kitchen was painted yellow and had a rooster and chicken wallpaper border around the ceiling. The breakfast table was wooden, and the chairs had pillows and seats matching the wallpaper.

"Max, I'm gonna cook a hot dog for lunch. You want one?" Ed asked.

"No, I ate at Mama and Daddy's earlier and I still feel stuffed."

Doris poured lemonade, and I watched Ed take two hot dogs and split them down the middle with a knife. He put a dab of butter in a pan and turned the heating element on the stove on high. In a few minutes, the salty smell of hot dogs filled the kitchen.

"That does smell good," I said.

"Max, just say the word if you want one."

"No, really, I don't, but they do smell good. It reminds me of the lunch counter at Woolworth's."

"Yeah?" Ed said. "That's where I got the idea. Been making mine this way for twenty or thirty years. Your daddy used to take you to Woolworth's in Thomasville to eat?"

"No, Aunt Ophelia used to take me and Doug when she'd baby sit. I just really did enjoy going there and eating those hot dogs."

"Max, I sure am sorry about your Aunt Ophelia," Doris said. "That woman was one of the strongest women I ever met. She'd lived a long time and had been through a lot with all those fiancés. I remember Ophelia helping my own parents with an old aunt of mine who was sick. She was always helping someone. It's just a shame to see someone like her pass and no one to pick up where she left off, no one to take over helping. Now old people just go to nursing homes and wait to die. It's sad."

"Yes, it is," I said.

"How's Doug?" Ed asked. "You knew he used to work for us when he was younger, didn't you, Max?" Ed gobbled both hot dogs in what seemed like two bites.

"No, I didn't know that. I recalled he worked on some different farms to make money in high school, but we drifted a little as we got older."

"He used to have a crush on Jaden," Ed said.

"Really? Jaden never mentioned that to me."

"I don't know that she knew. She was always reading and in her own world, but I could see it in Doug's eyes, the way he looked at her."

I laughed. Ed was right. Jaden did seem to be a bit of a space cadet from time to time, but she was smart. Certainly smarter than me. "Doug has had some problems, but I saw him this morning. He had to be put in rehab in Thomasville for alcohol and drugs, but he had a conversion experience, and I really believe he'll be okay."

"What happened?" Ed asked.

"He said he saw a light, saw Aunt Ophelia, and felt better than he could remember feeling. Said he was going to church Sunday when he got out."

"Bless his heart," said Doris and handed me a glass of lemonade and sat at the table.

"Well," Ed said. "I've heard about those kinds of experiences. I don't know what to make of them, but I hope he does straighten up. He's got potential."

"Did you all hear about the Yates family? Mama and Daddy told me this morning, and I was completely shocked. I need to call Jaden and tell her. I think she was friends with one of the Yates' daughters."

"I called and told her when it happened. I think she sent a card," Doris said.

"She didn't even mention that to me," I said.

"Did you know them?" Ed asked.

"I knew them in school, but I was never really close to them. Still, I would like to have known something about it."

"Jaden probably just didn't think about telling you, but she told me she wasn't surprised. She'd been over there and had seen some things happen that shocked her," Doris said.

"Like what?" I asked.

"Oh, I don't remember specifically, but it was the way their father talked to them. Little things he said and actions, too. Once Jaden told me that, I wouldn't let her go over there anymore. I told her those kids could come over here and spend the night anytime she wanted them to. They never did, though. Max, I did hear that their mama joined the church after it happened."

"That's what Mama and Daddy said."

"I think that's great that she joined. You know, we just don't go as much as we used to, but I still hear things. Your mama say anything about a rumor?"

"Yes," I said. "And I just don't think Daddy believes it. Stuff like that worries him."

"Nothing he can do about it," said Ed.

"That's true," said Doris. "No one is going to blame him for being the head deacon who hired him. You just never know what people are gonna do; they make their own choices."

A knock on the screen door at the back of the house revealed one of the farm hands. I could see him through the screen, but didn't know him. Ed went to the door.

"Everything's ready to go," he said.

"I'll be out there in a few minutes," said Ed.

"Ed, why don't you just stay and visit and let them handle it? One of these days you won't be able to keep working so hard. Keep it up and you won't even get to spend time with our grandbaby."

Ed and I laughed, and then, Ed said, "I will when Max and Jaden move home and take over the farming, so I can kick back." Ed winked at me, and Doris turned and just smiled a real sweet smile, the kind of smile she had when Jaden and I married several years ago, and while I couldn't see my own facial expression, I assumed it was probably shock. I had never done any farming, but I did have experience in management, and at the moment, I just couldn't fathom the thought of farming.

Ed went out the screen door, and Doris sipped her lemonade. I had already finished mine. "Max, you want some more lemonade?"

"No thanks," I said. "I need to get going. I am going to do some work on my computer today over at Aunt Ophelia's."

"You staying there?"

"Yes, Daddy suggested I stay there."

"Good thing you are. There's been some robberies when people die. It's a shame, but I guess they read the obituaries and then stake out a house when the funeral is going on. It is a novel way to commit a crime, if you think about it."

"Sure is, but I can't believe someone would do that."

"Me neither, but times are changing."

"Jaden wanted me to see if you had any peaches put up, so she could make some pies at the school luncheon they have at the end of the year."

"Oh yeah, Max. I almost forgot. I put them in a crate in the foyer along with some fresh peaches for you to take. When are you leaving?"

"I think I'll leave Sunday after church. I promised Doug I would go with him on Sunday."

"Well, maybe we'll see you there," Doris said.

"I guess I'll get going." We both stood and walked into the foyer and I picked up the small crate. Doris opened the door and walked with me out to the car. "Sure is hot out here. I don't know that I could ever get used to this heat again if we were to move back."

"You could adjust. People can adjust to just about anything."

I opened the trunk to the Cherokee and set the crate in. I thought how good the vehicle would smell for the ride home. Doris and I hugged, said goodbye, and I got in the Cherokee. I looked over toward the peach shed, Ed waved, and I waved back. I drove down the driveway, past the wagon wheel mailbox, and onto Egg and Butter Road.

I enjoyed Ed and Doris. They were hard working, salt of the earth people who never talked a lot, but what impressed me most was the way they unconditionally accepted others, including me. I felt sure they hated that I took their only child and daughter to Nashville, Tennessee, that we lived in a condo, that Jaden taught in a school with security officers, that we rarely came home, but they never complained about it, at least not that I was aware.

Chapter
5

When I pulled in the driveway at Aunt Ophelia's house, I knew I should take the peaches in as they would ruin in the vehicle. I rested for a while on the sofa downstairs and decided I should check my email from work. When I logged in, I deleted all the junk from the inbox, and though I constantly right clicked to block the junk emails, somehow they were able to bypass the block by re-sending the same junk through a different address. Then, I saw it. The email was from the owner, it was marked as important, addressed to everyone, and the title was "Restructure of the Organization."

At first, I simply glanced at the email and didn't think much about it, but then I reread it more slowly. While the message from Mr. Sampson simply announced a new vice president had been hired, and that even more changes would be made, I felt this new guy must be connected to Sampson from a political standpoint, since we didn't have an opening, a position, for a vice president. I knew Sampson well enough to know that nothing was simple, and the hiring of a new vice president meant the money to pay him could not cut into current profit for the Sampson family, that someone would get cut out of the picture in order to get needed funds to pay for his salary. The email casually mentioned something about restructuring and I had to wonder what that meant.

I felt sick to my stomach. I'd felt pretty close to Sampson and felt I should have known about any change in structure. I was in his inner circle and had done everything he had asked or suggested, though I didn't necessarily agree with him. I'd even given several hundred dollars to the Democratic Party at his suggestion when I was not a Democrat, but a free-floating voter, and Jaden would have had a fit had she known since she and her family religiously voted Republican. We had been over to Sampson and Earline's house several times for parties to watch the University of Tennessee games, even though neither one of us had gone to the University, and to family parties on holidays when we didn't travel to Pavo. Earline felt a commitment to us since we were not from Nashville, being outsiders, and didn't want us to spend holidays alone eating at restaurants. I had always sensed Sampson a puppet being controlled by the strings of Earline, whose father had owned the hotel, but when one works for someone or a group of people, he has to get with the program, join in whatever keeps him working. It seemed to me that it was like being a member of a certain religion, that once converted, you couldn't stray without fear of retribution, not from God, but from the people.

What irritated me most, however, was that Sampson hadn't mentioned anything to me, and I was the general manager with a supposed direct line to owner/president Sampson, and if anyone had been deserving of appointment to vice president status, it would have been me. After all, he had consulted me on practically everything about the business. I had even served on the Chamber of Commerce board and the noon Rotary of downtown Nashville, and I had even served on several committees, having been asked by the Mayor at Rotary. Most of all, I had turned the hotel business around by offering discounts, doing more marketing to groups, offering shuttles to the Ryman, Grand Ole Opry, international airport, major businesses, and I had improved room quality and trained staff more than ever had been done in the hotel's history. Even when it was difficult to get staff to work the third floor, or get customers to stay there because of the haunting, I created a marketing scheme that made the third floor the most popular in the hotel. What happened was a prostitute had leaped to her death decades before, and people had seen the ghostly apparition of a woman wearing a gown caked with blood and heard screams, doors slamming, and moaning. I had read that the notorious gangster Al Capone often stopped in Tennessee on runs between Chicago and Florida at a house he owned in Monteagle. The owners had turned the place into a popular restaurant, and they had capitalized on the home's criminal history. Jaden and I had dinner there one weekend after hiking the Fiery Gizzard trail on the mountain. It had also been rumored that Capone stayed in Nashville some, as well prior to, or after owning the house in Monteagle, so I did a little research at the state archives and learned he'd stayed in the hotel. Then, using a little imagination, I turned the suicidal woman on the third floor into yet another lover in a river of jilted lovers of Al Capone and ended up with a new marketing strategy that worked. What was really interesting to me was seeing the story grow on its own over a year or so until people requested to be housed on the third floor, hoping for a glance at Al Capone and his jilted lover's apparitions, and to my surprise, housekeeping employees actually wanted to be assigned to that floor. Whether I believed in ghosts or not, which I tended not to believe in, I wouldn't deny others the experience of them.

All of my work had yielded a huge profit for Sampson and nice bonuses for me, and these had continued through the years Jaden and I had been in Nashville. The hiring of a new vice president meant that I would report to him, and the interesting thing was that the new guy had not been in the tourism industry at all. In fact, he had worked for Eddie Kovacs, a developer who I knew from Rotary. Kovacs was a shrewd man who purchased buildings, reconfigured them into expensive condos, or bulldozed buildings for construction of new buildings. In fact, Kovacs had reconfigured an old warehouse downtown for the condo building Jaden and I lived in, and he had done a meticulous job. I imagined Kovacs to be a grown-up kid who had been alienated by his parents and spent all his time in his room with Legos. He had a fast-talking Yankee accent, hailing from New Jersey, and though he was nice enough at Rotary the few times I had sat at his table and talked with him, he was not interested in people. He talked superficially—weather, events in the city, the New York Yankees. Even during the Pledge of Allegiance, the Rotary four-way test, the lunch prayer, and the guest speaker every week, I watched Eddie and knew his mind was elsewhere, the wheels constantly turning and clicking like a master clock from Switzerland, and scanning the audience at Rotary for any females who might be new and could fall victim to his predatory ways, which he had become so successful at by his fast-talking masculinity and seemingly endless supply of cash that provides someone a false feeling of security. Eddie's double-breasted suits, his hundred dollar haircuts and gel, his shined shoes by the old black man downtown on the corner, and his diamond cufflinks signified his importance to others. I simply saw him as a man looking to make yet another dollar and using any means to do so. If the new vice president was Kovacs' protégé, then I knew I could be civil toward him, but not necessarily like him, and I also knew my job might be in danger.

I also suspected Sampson might be looking at retirement, selling out the business, spending part of his time at their condo in Destin, Florida, particularly in the winter when his arthritis inflamed his body and made him resemble the Tin Man from "The Wizard of Oz." When gout would inflame his toe joints for a few days, he would drive their customized white van with orange pin stripes to signify his dedication to the University of Tennessee, which he had attended only briefly in his youth. He would move into the motorized buggy and glide down the automatic handicapped ramp and zoom through the lobby into the restaurant, where he would down steak and eggs at breakfast, totally ignoring his doctor's orders to stay away from red meat.

Part of me had even looked at Sampson as a surrogate father. He had often called me "his boy," and I suppose what made him like me so much was he had never had a son of his own. I didn't want to believe it was the money I'd help him make. He did have two step-daughters from Earline's earlier marriage to a Tennessee congressman, who ended up in jail for taking bribes from undercover agents for votes on bills. It had apparently been a dark cloud in Tennessee politics, but it had not been the first and I felt sure it would not be the last.

I knew I needed to call Jaden, but I didn't want to bother her at school. I knew this restructuring could affect my position, but I wasn't worried. If I wanted another job in Nashville, I would get it, and I wasn't too worried about finances either if restructuring meant losing my position. Jaden and I had saved a lot of money over the years, and we had always lived within our means. Coming from families who once had money but no longer had money meant we had been conditioned to save. In fact, our rule was to live only on one of our paychecks. That way, if one of us lost a job, or God forbid, something happened to one of us, we could survive.

Still, knowing all this did not help the way I felt. What I wanted to do was call some old friends, go out, and have a drink. I knew I couldn't call Doug since he was recovering, and I also remembered the few times we'd gone out together. Once, when we were in high school, and Doug was sixteen and I was fifteen, there was a party for juniors and seniors at Pavo High in Thomasville at one of the motels. We had both been invited, so we got a couple of dates. Doug's date was Reba, the Church of Christ preacher's daughter, who was only fourteen. My date was the Methodist minister's daughter, who was my age. In addition, our friend Sam, who was the Baptist preacher's son, went without a date. Doug and Sam drove their vehicles, since I did not own a car until halfway through my sixteenth year.

The seniors had rented three rooms at the Sheraton that had connecting doors. Music was blasting, mainly Lynyrd Skynyrd's "Free Bird." Even today, that song brings a warm feeling over me when I hear it in the Jeep and I turn it up. I don't know if the warm feeling is the fondness I feel for the music or from the memory of all the beer I consumed that makes one feel warm on a cold night. Sam didn't consume beer, though. He had crept into the bathroom where all the beer, wine, and liquor were iced down in the tub. He'd pulled a fifth of Jack Daniel's out of the ice, opened the bottle, and turned it straight up, downing the entire fifth. Everyone had cheered him on, and even in my half-inebriated state, I felt this was the beginning of a bad night. Shortly after, Sam became really drunk and began wild dancing, running, and cursing on the hotel's second floor balcony. He'd even yelled at some tourists and stuck his head through the metal railing on the balcony. It took several of us to get his head back through the railing, and because we were laughing so hard, he began to curse and get violent toward us.

The motel management had received numerous complaints, so we were asked to leave. It was bad enough all lied and said we were going to see a movie in Thomasville, but with Sam in such a state, I had a feeling it would only get worse, and it did. Sam got in his car, began doing doughnuts in the parking lot, leaving smoke from the rubber burning on the asphalt. When he finally stopped, he was sick, throwing up inside his car and all over himself. He even urinated and defecated on himself. Finally, Sam passed out. Doug and I had hatched a plan to cover ourselves. The plan had been that I would drive Sam's car home—even though I had a learner's permit—and pull the car into the front yard of the Baptist pastorium. Then I'd get out and jump into Doug's car with our dates, and we would tell everyone Sam had left the movies and when he returned, he was drunk, and we didn't know what else to do but take him home. We got Sam into the backseat and implemented our plan.

As I had driven down the highway toward Pavo, music off and windows down, I felt okay. When I'd glanced in the rearview mirror, Doug was following closely behind, so a cop wouldn't see me driving and pull me over, which could have easily happened had they seen me driving. The best and worst thing about a small town is that everyone knows everyone else. In times like this, it can be devastating, but in other times, it can be the best thing ever to know everyone. I heard movement in the backseat and low, guttural sounds that reminded me of a horror movie. Then I saw Sam in the rear-view mirror. He had risen from his drunken stupor and had an insane look on his face. He'd grabbed me from behind by the throat and choked me. As I swerved from one side of the road to the other, I tried to yell, which came out as a strained whisper, and Sam fell motionless in the backseat. With Sam passed out again, I coughed and breathed until I felt some-what normal, and when I saw the "Welcome to Pavo" sign, I inhaled and exhaled deeply, feeling relief.

Turning from Main onto Elm, I had driven below the speed limit with Doug still following close behind. As we rounded a curve and approached Sam's house, I noticed what I thought were people standing in the minister's front yard, and unfortunately, I was accurate in my assumption. Of all things, the minister and his wife were having a prayer party, which had just ended. There seemed to be about forty people in their front yard, getting ready to leave. As I drove slowly by, they all waved, thinking it was Sam, but I saw the looks on their puzzled faces when they caught a glimpse of me at the wheel thanks to the streetlights. I waved back and kept on driving until I reached Miss Parker's house, a young school teacher who had been rumored to sleep with senior football players and buy them beer. Her front porch light was on, and Doug eased in behind me. I knocked on the door, and when she opened the door, she stood dressed in her robe and said, "Hey Max."

"Hey," I said. "Do you mind if I use your phone?" Then, I offered the first of my series of lies. "We've all been to the movies in Thomasville, and Sam came back after it was over really drunk. I need to call his parents. He's passed out in the backseat, and Doug and our dates are in Doug's car." I wanted to add that, so she wouldn't have the impression I was using a line to come in for a sleepover, not that I thought she would since I wasn't a football player and was actually kind of scrawny. Years later, I still wondered if the rumors of the teacher were true, or if football players started the rumor, so other students would think they were getting laid.

"Oh my," she said. "Come on in."

I used the phone and dialed the number. Back then, one had to only dial the last four digits, and the minister's wife answered on the second ring.

"Mrs. Vickers," I said. "We went to the movies and Sam came back to get us and he was drunk. He's pretty sick. He's in the backseat passed out."

"Bring him home right now!" she yelled.

"Yes ma'am," I said.

I thanked Ms. Parker and she told me to be careful. As I walked out the front door, she told me to come back and visit some time, that she always liked me. I nodded, went out, and got back in Sam's car. The dried vomit smell in Sam's car was even more overpowering than it had been driving down the road with the wind blowing in, and I felt a little nauseated, since it reminded me of spaghetti sauce.

As I pulled into the driveway at Sam's house, his parents were there to meet me, and the prayer crowd had dissipated. Then, I told the second round of lies. I had explained about the movie, his getting drunk and coming back to get us, but I could tell they didn't buy it. I knew they were concerned about their son, but I also had half-way hoped for some gratitude. After all, I didn't have to drive him home, nearly getting choked to death.

I hopped into Doug's car and we drove away, looking back and watching them try to lug him out of the car. I told them what I told Ms. Parker and the Rev. and Mrs. Vickers. I told them to stick to the story, that no matter what happened, we all needed to be on the same page.

We dropped the girls off first. I remember it felt like a date gone bad, so we didn't kiss them goodnight; we just said goodnight. When I got home, Mama and Daddy were already in bed, but their reading lamps were on. I opened the door and found Mama reading her Sunday school lesson.

"Hey Max. Did ya'll enjoy the movie?"

"Yes, but there was a problem."

Mama elbowed Daddy, his eyes opened, and he sat up. "Sam didn't go to the movies with us, but he came back when it was over to pick us up. He was really drunk."

"Lord, have mercy," Mama blurted out.

I told them about the vomit and all, told them how I drove him home, but when we got to his house, they were having a prayer party, and I drove a little further down the road and used Ms. Parker's phone. Mama raised her eyebrows when I said that. I suspected she had heard about Ms. Parker, but she didn't say anything about it. I told them about the Rev. and Mrs. Vickers and taking Sam home.

"Well, you did the right thing," Daddy told me. "Try to get some sleep. I'm sure Sam and his parents will be all right."

All Mama echoed was, "Lord, have mercy."

I had gone on to bed, but tossed and turned a lot. I heard the phone ring about three in the morning, and heard Daddy answer. "Well, that's not what Max told us, and I don't believe he'd lie about it."

I laid in bed and felt guiltier than I ever had before. My chest hurt and I struggled to breathe. I continued to toss and turn the rest of the night and couldn't stop thinking about my having lied. I felt clammy and sick to my stomach.

When we got to church the next morning, everyone knew—another characteristic of small town life is the grapevine. Some looked at me with scolding looks, and others came up to me and told me they had heard what I had done to help Sam. For the first time since Reverend Vickers had begun preaching at First Baptist, he didn't yell, or beat, on the podium. Instead, he looked defeated.

Sam sat next to his mother on the first row and looked ashen. He didn't speak at all. At the end of the service, when the church began singing "I Surrender All," I saw people staring at Sam and felt like some people might be staring at me in the same way, but no one had gone down to join the church or rededicate themselves, so they stopped on the third verse, a first as I recall.

On Monday, the school had been abuzz with the story, and it had stretched to Sam having his stomach pumped, his car having been totaled by me, me having been arrested for driving without a license, a lawsuit from the motel owner for damages, all the ministers in Pavo crusading against the sale of alcohol for starters.

After a few days, things calmed, but never totally disappeared. Mama and Daddy had acted standoffish towards me, and after three days, Daddy addressed the situation at the supper table. "Max, did you lie?"

"Yes, sir," I replied, but if he had really counted, it would have been a lot more than one.

"You know I don't care that you drank. I think what you did for Sam was a good deed. But I have always taught you not to lie to me. The truth is far easier to deal with than a lie on top of the truth. I want you to always tell me the truth, and we'll work it out one way or another."

Tears had welled in my eyes and a lump formed in my throat, probably the first since my early childhood, and I made a promise I would not lie to them again, and I haven't. Reverend Vickers resigned the following month, and they moved away. I never knew what became of Sam, but I felt he would be okay. Daddy headed the search committee for a new preacher.

Chapter
6

I was still worried about my job, but I decided I wouldn't go out drinking as it could lead to trouble. I didn't need any more trouble. Besides, I thought I was too old for partying. I did try to reach Jaden, but couldn't. I assumed she was running errands or working late. Since they'd instituted yet another bureaucratic policy in the school system, that was more of a paperwork nightmare than anything else, she and the other teachers had worked more for no additional pay. Though I had never really thought about it while I was in school, or even college, I realized that those who teach do so for the love of it as opposed to the pay. At least that's how it should be, but that, too, is the distinction between a good teacher and a bad teacher, and there were plenty of bad ones. In fact, some continued to teach and scar young minds because they probably couldn't get another job anyway.

Aunt Ophelia's doorbell rang, and it surprised me for a moment. I figured it had to be my parents or Jaden's parents, but I didn't think they would actually ring the bell. When I went down the stairs, I could see a hefty policeman standing at the screen door.

As I neared the screen door, the raspy voice said, "Hey Max. I heard you were in town."

I unlocked the latch and opened the door. "Buddy, good to see you." We shook hands and I invited him into the living room, though he didn't take a seat.

"I'm real sorry to hear about your aunt."

"Thanks. We will miss her, but it was her time."

"I was working, and actually, I was leading the funeral. I didn't know if you knew it was me in the police car or not."

"I didn't know," I said, and remembered seeing a police car leading the funeral procession, stopping where the roads cross on the way to the cemetery, and a policeman getting out, taking his hat off as the cars passed. "We appreciate it," I added.

Buddy nodded. "How's Jaden?"

"She's doing fine. She couldn't come though, because she's teaching and couldn't get a substitute."

"You staying a while?"

"No, I'm heading back to Nashville tomorrow after church. It takes about seven or eight hours to get home."

"Your Aunt Ophelia has a nice place out here," Buddy commented.

"It is peaceful. That's probably why she had such a long life." We both laughed.

"I hate to ask this so soon, but are ya'll going to sell the place?"

"Why do you ask?"

"Me and Miriam have four kids, you know, and we've outgrown our trailer. We've been wanting to buy a place, but with me being a policeman and her being a waitress at the café downtown, we've never been able to afford much. Miriam's daddy passed a few months back, and her mama shouldn't be staying by herself because she's got diabetes real bad. We were thinking about buying a bigger place, an old place maybe we could fix up. The trailer's paid for, and it's sitting on a few acres. I think I know someone who would buy it for a good price. Be a good down payment on a place like this."

I listened to Buddy, and though I felt sorry for him and I admired him for thinking, since so many people don't really think through such decisions, I knew we wouldn't sell Aunt Ophelia's place. It had been in the family for a long time and was part of the Peacock history, the legacy.

"I don't think my daddy wants to sell it, but if he does, you'll get first dibs since you're the only one who's asked that I know of."

"I appreciate that Max. Should I talk to your father?"

"I'll mention it to him. He may even call you one way or another, if for no other reason than to invite you to church."

Buddy laughed. "Your mom and dad are still pretty active in the church, aren't they?"

"Yes," I said. "Daddy is still the head deacon."

"I figured as much. I've heard they got some trouble brewing about the preacher and Mrs. Yates."

"Oh, yeah? I heard there was a rumor going around, but, Buddy, that doesn't surprise me none. There's always rumors going around here."

"Maybe so, but I suspect this is more than a rumor. That Mrs. Yates needed some attention, and it looks like she got it. I worked that scene. I shouldn't tell you this, so don't tell nobody, but you should have seen her husband. She shot him first in his private area and he laid there on the floor for a long time bleeding and suffering before she finally finished him off. I think she lectured him a while. Then, she called us. She was real matter-of-fact about it. Said something like 'I have shot and killed my husband, and somebody needs to come out here and get him. Take him to the funeral home or something. I want to clean up the kitchen.' I was first out there, and when I got there, she was just mumbling and whispering, sounded like cursing under her breath, and sitting at the table with the gun laying right there."

"That's an odd reaction, it seems to me. Some people are just crazy, but I guess Mr. Yates was pretty abusive."

"Oh yeah, he was, but unless a wife files a formal complaint, there's not a lot we can actually do. Remember that pharmacist who killed his pharmacist tech down in Tallahassee? She wouldn't give in to his desires, so he had his way with her against her will, killed her, chopped her up and buried her out there near the lake. When they were doing work on that dam, they unearthed her body. It'd been twenty years and all the time the family was thinking she'd run off some where and he'd been covering it up for years, still getting away with God knows what. Since Mrs. Yates joined the church though, that preacher has been out there a lot. I believe he had visited with them before Mrs. Yates killed her husband. One thing about Rev. Mason is that he'll really go where the trouble is and try to bring whatever is going on to a stop."

"Yeah, he's a good minister. Speaking of rumors, do you remember that rumor about Big Foot out in the woods behind the school?"

"Yeah, we must have been seniors. Everyone was talking about having seen a creature. Then a couple of teachers claimed they'd seen it, too. The news people out of Albany and Tallahassee came over and interviewed us. Then, those crazy river rats went missing for a day or two, and the story just kept getting bigger. People really thought Big Foot had them kids, and all the time they were just skipping school and playing out in those pine woods."

"Buddy, why did they call those kids river rats?"

"They lived out by the river and lived like rats. Their family members rummaged through every dumpster in the county. Plus the kids looked like they'd been in the river; their hair was always so greasy and wet-looking."

I shook my head. "That's a shame. Whatever happened to those people?"

"I don't know. I thought I saw one some time back working over in Valdosta at the super Wal-Mart, but I didn't say nothing."

"Well, how are your kids?"

"They are all fine. Buddy Junior is in middle school now, playing sports. He's addicted to sports, but it's better than being addicted to meth or crack or something."

"Are drugs really that bad here? I know they have pockets in Nashville, but I don't think it's too bad there."

"Well, when you've got poverty and the parents don't really care, it's easy for them to get into something that leads to something more serious. Just last week, we worked a wreck where the mama was on meth and her two kids were killed. They were from Camilla, but it was a shame. Right now, the mama is in rehab, but she stands to be charged for murder. Some say she'll get off because having her kids get killed is punishment enough for her, but I believe she'll serve some time."

"She ought to. How are your other kids?"

"We've got Misty and Christy, the twins—they're in fifth grade and look just like their mama, thank God, and last is Hunter. He's in first grade, a bit on the shy side, but I think I was, too, when I was a kid. You and Jaden have kids?"

"No, we haven't. We've been talking about it some."

"You do know talking isn't going to get you a kid, right? You don't need to wait too long or you won't have the energy. I'm telling you it takes a lot of energy to keep up and do everything that needs to be done."

We both laughed.

"I better get on back. School will be out soon, and traffic will pick-up." I thought about his traffic and assumed it was Buddy's way of saying goodbye, since traffic really never picked up in Pavo.

"Buddy, whatever happened to the logger who hit Aunt Ophelia?"

"I don't know. He was from over around Waycross. He was all broken up about hitting her, but she weaved in his lane and he couldn't avoid it. Had no priors on him at all. He said his only comfort was that she had a smile on her face and seemed peaceful. He didn't even think she was dead because she didn't appear hurt. The one thing that puzzled him was that he thought there were two people in her car. He thought it was an old man, but when he got out of the truck and went to the car, it was just her. I think he was probably just confused and dazed a bit, but to appease his insistence, we did search the immediate area just in case. Nothing turned up."

"I appreciate you telling me it was peaceful for her. It does mean a lot. That's odd about the fellow seeing someone else with her. I doubt anyone would have been with her."

We shook hands again, and Buddy opened the squeaky screen door. I went out behind him, and no sooner had we stepped on the porch than we heard rattling. Buddy reached in his pocket, brought out a big pocketknife, flipped it open, and eased down the steps and into the yard. He moved slowly around the azaleas toward the curled Diamondback Rattler under the porch swing. I didn't say a word, but what I wanted to tell Buddy was just to shoot the damned snake. Though he was a lot bigger than I ever recall him being, Buddy moved like lightning. The snake had kept its attention on me and never turned toward Buddy who came up behind, grabbed the snake with his left hand just below the head, cut it off with his right hand, slung it into the bushes, and dropped the snake's body on the porch floor. The now dead snake flipped and flopped and grew more still with each passing minute.

"Why didn't you just shoot him?"

"You never know what might happen when you shoot a gun. If you miss, he'd be on you with one jump. I've seen 'em jump twice their length. The bullet could ricochet, too, and end up hurting one of us. My daddy taught me to kill a snake this way and it don't bother me none."

"That's amazing. He's gotta be four feet long."

"He's probably a little over four feet. If you don't mind, I'd like to keep him."

"What in the world for?"

"Oh, I'll dry him for a day or two, and then I'll get his skin off and make a belt. Make a nice Christmas gift for Buddy Junior."

"You want me to get you a grocery bag or something to put him in?"

"Sure."

I went back in, grabbed a plastic trash bag, and brought it out, handing it to Buddy. He raked the flopping snake in the bag with his boots. The head he'd tossed in the azaleas, and he cautioned me not to go in the azaleas given that the poisonous fangs could still hurt me. "It's dog days now. Snakes are blind. He had a film covering his eyes, so they are crawling and will strike a moving target even more than usual. Don't worry about the head. Ants'll eat him in a day or two," he added.

Buddy tied the bag, walked to his patrol car, and tossed it in the trunk. He came back to the porch and asked if I minded if he washed his hands.

"Sure, the bathroom is down the hall, on the right under the stairs."

Finished washing and back on the porch, Buddy and I walked to his car. I told him it was good to see him, and he said the same. I told him I would talk with my daddy and he would call him about the house. He got in and drove off and I walked back toward the porch, scanning the ground for other snakes. One thing about snakes is that they are a part of southern living, and no matter what people do to avoid them, they show up periodically.

Once I got back inside, the phone rang. I answered on the third ring. "Something wrong, Max?"

"No, why?"

"Somebody said the police were out there. After you didn't answer right away, I told your Daddy we were going to have to come out there."

"Buddy stopped by to visit a moment and ask about whether we were going to sell Aunt Ophelia's house."

"Well, I wouldn't mind selling it. I could use a new car, but I don't think your daddy wants to sell it. He wants you and Jaden to move back and live there. Of course, I do too, but I don't know how I'm gonna get me a new car." I could always count on Mama being up front and honest.

"I'll have to talk with Jaden about moving."

"I know you do. Well, are you still coming to church tomorrow? Dorine called and said Doug was planning on it. Ya'll can come over after and we'll have a big lunch."

"I'll need to get on the road pretty quick. I'd like to get back before dark."

"You can't drive that far without eating something."

"You're right, Mama. I'll be there. See you tomorrow." We both said goodbye and hung up the phones.

Mama was always worried about people eating. It was a wonder I wasn't fat, given all the food I consumed over the years and even more of a wonder I didn't have arteries swimming in sludge, given the fried greasy food we ate, but I tried to change my eating habits since Jaden and I had been married. In fact, when we went out to eat in Nashville, we loved exploring different restaurants downtown and in the Green Hills area where most of the country music stars lived, and in the West End community, where Vanderbilt was located. Those areas had the more posh and health-conscious restaurants.

Thinking about the good food in Nashville made my stomach rumble, and since Mama hadn't asked me to come over for dinner, I decided to drive over to Thomasville and eat at the Tasty World restaurant. I don't know why, really. There were far better places to eat in Thomasville, but occasionally, the Tasty World conjured olfactory images and fond memories of people for me because of all the time I spent working there. Tasty World was part of the motel where I had worked for years that helped me get a jump start on a career. The motel/restaurant also had outside gas pumps and a gift shop, that mainly sold cheap items made in China for high retail prices—items like rubber snakes, glitter globes with the Disney castle, and alligator-shaped ceramic ashtrays. A PacMan game had been in the corner along with a pin-ball machine. I had become quite the PacMan master in those years, and I wondered if the machine was still there. Prior to my moving up to motel clerk, I had bussed tables in the Tasty World and later was promoted to dishwasher. I had even been temporarily promoted to cook, but had been quickly demoted back to dishwasher given the number of cooking orders I had ruined. The most important memories were of the people, the good times and laughs we had shared.

I recalled Lula—everyone pronounced her name Luler— the black cook who lived way out of town in the swamplands of Thomas County. She had driven a twenty-year-old Buick Skylark with rusting paint, balding tires, and a worn-out engine. Frequently, the busboys or dishwashers would give Lula a ride home when her car would not run. Many of them knew she was afraid of ghosts, and to get to her house, we had to pass the eeriest cemetery at a Primitive Baptist Church that was rumored to have been haunted. One of the other busboys or dishwashers would yell, "Look-a-there, Lula. It's a woman floating in the cemetery," and Lula would pull her stained white apron over her head, yelling, "Lawd, Lawd. Protect me, Lawd." They would all laugh, and I did, too, initially, but it seemed to be an old joke to me after the first time. Plus, I always thought about someone doing that to me and how I would feel.

I wondered how many of my friends from that time were still alive, still working there. The owner, Larry, who was from India and in country on a green card or work visa, flashed in my mind. Larry's real name was Kaushal, and he was a clever fellow. Small in stature, he was thin, almost emaciated, probably because he didn't eat the same foods we ate, and had a quick gate. His black hair was oily and parted on the side, and he wore knit pants and silk shirts, even after the silk shirts had gone out of style shortly after the Saturday Night Fever with John Travolta craze. Though I felt sure Larry still owned the motel operation, I wondered about the clothes he was now wearing and if he could pronounce words any better. R's seemed the problem for his conversion from Indian to American English, which is why I always wondered why he chose Larry as his American name. The R's sounded more like W's, making his name sound like "Lawwie." Once I asked why he didn't use his real name, and he said, "Americans no understand." I actually think people would have preferred him not pretending to be an American when he wasn't, much like recently when I needed technical support for my home computer and had been routed to India where I talked with Sam, Bill, and Henry, none of whom were really named that and still came up with no solution to that particular computer problem, though my credit card was still charged.

I also wondered about Jeff, who everyone called Junior. Jeff had been a busboy/dishwasher, too, and was the son of the manager Jeff, Sr., a chain-smoking fellow, who instead of answering his calls "Hello" would answer, "Yell-ow." He didn't have a speech impediment or lisp, but I'd heard he had some oral surgery in his youth that impacted his speech development. I figured it had something to do with his dentures, which would periodically slip around, causing him to contort his face until they were in place again. Jeff Junior never got in trouble because he lied his way out of everything. Once he had taken a rubber snake from the gift shop and hid it under the bags of bread in the storage area beneath the stainless steel grill. Lula had been cutting onions with a butcher knife, tossing them on the grill, and dousing them in melted butter as part of a steak meal when she reached under the grill to pull out a bag of Texas toast. The rubber snake fell on her white tennis shoes, she screamed, kicked the snake across the kitchen, and went running and screaming through the restaurant, all the while waving the butcher knife. The restaurant was full, and people dropped their forks and spoons. Jeff Junior, the waitresses, and me had all guffawed at the incident, but when we saw the cloud of smoke moving toward the kitchen, we knew Jeff Senior was marching to bark reprimands. Of course, Jeff Junior didn't know how the rubber snake got there, and no one else would confess for him. Lula finally calmed, but she wouldn't speak to any of us the rest of the shift, even knowing it was Jeff Junior who had done the deed.

Chapter
7

I hadn't been to the motel and Tasty World in several years. Mostly when Jaden and I had come home to visit, we visited relatives, and it always struck me as odd that from birth to death, we tend to become so close to people, yet when we move on, we tend to lose touch with those who had helped shape who we had become. When I pulled into the parking lot of the motel and Tasty World, the first thing that stunned me was the name change. Tasty World had become the Thomasville Grill, and although the parking lot had been resurfaced, new paint outlined parking spaces, and some new landscaping, the brick buildings seemed the same, except for the new architectural shingled roof.

I didn't recognize anyone immediately as I entered. The high school hostess seated me, and I was impressed with the new look of the former Tasty World. The Thomasville Grill had round wooden tables, new chairs, and new carpet, a dark hunter green and blue color with a diamond pattern, replacing the metal tables and red shag carpet I recalled. There were indoor plants in clay pots strategically located for ambiance and a variety of oldies blues music set the mood—songs by B.B. King, Muddy Waters, and Billie Holiday were a few of the ones I recognized. The light fixtures, too, had been re- placed. The inset lights—yellowed stained-glass imitations made of Plexiglas—had been replaced with chandeliers with torpedo and flame-shaped bulbs and miniature lamp shades. As I glanced at the menu, I noticed heart-healthy selections that were non-existent when I'd worked there, and the traditional and historical side salad and chef salad had been replaced with walnut and raspberry salad, marinated Caribbean salad, spinach, almond, and water chestnut salad. I opted for the latter. The carbonated soft drinks were there, of course, but the variety had increased. In addition, green tea was offered along with decaffeinated soft drinks, a rarity given the need for a society addicted to caffeine. The patty melt, a long time favorite, had been replaced with a few Reuben sandwiches, and there were a number of burgers, including turkey and soy, from which to select.

As the waitress approached, dressed in khakis and a white polo with a name tag pinned to the pocket, she looked more modern than the waitresses I had worked with who wore black skirts, colonial white blouses with ruffles, pantyhose, and white nursing shoes. While this waitress had a bobbed hair cut, styled with a dab of gel for hold, the former waitresses I remembered had netting to cover their hair. Times had certainly changed, and while we tend to think change is positive or good, it is simply change.

"Welcome to the Thomasville Grill. I'm Marianne and I'll be serving you today. What would you like to drink?"

"Caffeine-free diet Coke."

"Okay, I'll get that right out to you."

"You look familiar. I'm Max Peacock from Pavo. I used to work here. Do I know you?"

"No, but I know your name. My sister Kathy used to work here years ago while she was in college."

"Kathy Varns?"

"That's her. I remember the wreck you two were in on your first date."

I laughed. "I hadn't thought about that in years." But the whole event flashed in my mind quickly. The first—and last—date we had gone on, we had been driving in heavy traffic, skidded and hit the back end of a Cadillac. While the Cadillac had no damage, the Sirocco's front end had crunched, accordion-like, and the impact had been so hard that Kathy had gone through the windshield. There was no seat-belt law at that time. I had jumped out to survey the damage to my car, and only then did I notice Kathy's side of the windshield busted with hair dangling from the broken glass. Our date of dinner and a movie changed to an evening at Archbold Memorial Hospital's emergency room with her parents staring me down, and my mother repeating, "It could have been worse; thank the Lord it weren't."

Kathy was X-rayed, poked and prodded, but the diagnosis of a concussion wasn't too severe, and aside from a major headache, a lump on her forehead, and some disorientation, she turned out to be fine in a few days. We never went out again, thanks to her parents, but everyone at the motel had given me a hard time because I had been more concerned for my car, so she told everyone.

"Kathy never did forget. She and I were talking last week and she mentioned she'd heard you were living in Nashville running a big resort. I ought to call her on her cell and tell her you're here, but she's shopping at the mall in Tallahassee today with her son."

"We do live in Nashville. So, Kathy has a son? What's she doing these days?"

"She's a medical transcriptionist for a group of doctors here in town. She got divorced a few years ago and hasn't remarried. She caught her ex-husband, Bill, with another woman and finally ran him off, but I think they still see each other. Her son, Josh, is a cutie. Looks just like her when she was little. I see you're married."

"Yes, I've been married for some time now."

"Let me go get your Coke and I'll come back in a minute."

Marianne returned with my caffeine-free diet Coke. "Here you go, Max."

"I'm curious if anyone who used to work here when I did is still here."

"The former manager, Jeff, died a while back after a battle with cancer, which started in his gums, spread to his mouth and throat. His son, Jeff, Jr. trains hunting dogs for a plantation out near Monticello. Lula was the evening cook for a long time, but about two years ago, she went off the road near that Primitive Baptist church out from Pavo. She was disabled and hasn't spoken since her wreck. The owner, Larry, is still around, but he took on a new business partner from India who mostly does all the work now while he does some traveling."

"I didn't know all that. I'm sorry to hear that about Jeff and Lula." Part of me wondered about Lula having a wreck near the Primitive Baptist Church, if she'd seen something.

"There's one person here you might remember, Effie. Effie's still the breakfast and lunch cook. She's cut back on hours now, since she draws Social Security. Do you remember her?

"Sure, I do. Is she here today?"

"Yeah, I'll tell her you're out here. She'll probably give you extra portions."

"I don't need that."

"Be right back."

I watched Effie coming out of the kitchen. She hadn't gained weight, but her hair had grayed some and she had somewhat of a limp. She grinned and I could see a wide, white smile, except for the one gold tooth that glistened in the dim lighting of the Thomasville Grill. "Max, baby, how you doin'?"

I stood and gave her a big hug. "Good, Effie. It's good to see you. How're you doing?"

"Fine, I reckon. Don't do no good to complain anyway."

"That's true."

Effie pulled the chair out from under the table and slowly sat. "I'm tired, Max. Tired time comes 'round for everybody sooner or later. Time come for me 'bout two years ago now. Just can't hardly keep it up much longer, but I keep on going best I can." Effie pulled an L&M cigarette from her apron and lit it.

"You still smoking?"

"Yeah, doctor told me to quit. Blood pressure, heart beat skips like my old car that needs a tune-up, but I did cut back."

"How's your family?"

"That's what keeps me goin'. Got all three children married off and all three went to college. I'm so proud of them, and part of it's cause what you told me."

"What I told you?"

"You told me a long time ago to make 'em go whether they wanted to or not, that they wouldn't regret it. I didn't know what you meant cause I never went. Fact, nobody in my family ever went, but I kept after them to go. And they got most of it paid by the gov'ment. What it didn't pay, I took on extra work till they all got through. That's probably why I'm so tired. A body can only take so much 'fore it gives out."

"I'm proud of them, too." I honestly had no recollection of giving her any advice, however.

"Now they all gone off from here and will have a better life for it. I miss 'em, though. Know what I miss most, Max?"

"What's that?"

"I miss 'em when they was little, comin' and gettin' in bed with me and snugglin'. Ain't no better feelin' in the whole world. Now I'm all alone, but I got my memory. That helps."

"Why don't you go to college now?"

"You crazy?"

"No, it's free after you're sixty-five. Did you know that?"

"Lord, no, I didn't know that. But I never went to high school."

"You can get a G.E.D. by taking some night classes at the Board of Education here. Then take a test and when you get the G.E.D., you can go right to college."

Effie laughed. "I'll think about that. I'd be the oldest one there."

"Yeah, you probably would, but you'd do fine in history, since you remember most of it."

Effie laughed and I did, too.

"I'll tell you what, I'll think on it. I keep busy with the church, though. Old people's got to have something to keep them busy, or they just rot."

I nodded. "That's true."

"Max, how's life treatin' you? You still go to church?"

"Good. Jaden and I go to a church in Nashville, but it's a big church. I do kind of miss the closeness of a smaller church and community."

"Whatever you do, don't lose your religion. Beliefs change with time, but they still beliefs that need to be kept." Effie snuffed her cigarette out in the glass tray. "You like the big city life?"

"I think it's time to come home. With my great aunt Ophelia's passing, and mine and Jaden's parents getting older, we have thought about moving back. It's just that there's not a good job for me in this area."

Effie's eyes were focused. Both had a bluish film covering them, and I felt Effie could see right through my exterior. "If it's meant to be, God will lead you home."

"You may be right, Effie, but I wish I knew one way or another."

While part of me believed that was true, even though it bordered on the concept of predestination, I never quite understood it or thought much about it. It seemed Baptists leaned more toward the opposite side of that coin, free will.

"Grass ain't always greener on the other side, is it? You know that's true somewhere deep inside, and coming home don't mean you got to live in Pavo. You could just move closer. Find you a job nearby."

"You know, Effie, I hadn't really thought about that."

Effie smiled and looked toward the door where a large group was coming in for lunch. "I guess I need to get back to the kitchen. I got to get your lunch, anyway. You ought to look in Tallahassee. A cousin of mine works downtown, says their manager is leaving. It's that old hotel near the capitol."

"I know the place you're talking about. The Apalachee, right? I'll check it out. Thanks, Effie."

"Good to see you, Max. Don't be a stranger. Come by and visit more often."

"Will do." Effie stood, and I stood, too, and we hugged again.

Shortly, Marianne brought my salad, and I enjoyed almost every morsel, except for what I could not eat. Effie had given me more than enough, and though I was ready to go, I had the feeling I should undo my belt a notch or two before getting up for fear of splitting my pants.

Marianne returned. "You doing okay?"

"Too full," I said.

"Kathy told me about the cook, Lula, who got fired for stealing a whole ham one night, hiding it under her apron, and you begged the manger to give her, her job back, even agreeing to pay for the ham."

"I vaguely recall that, but it seems she had several kids and wasn't making that much and sometimes you do what you have to in order to get by."

"Kathy also told me about what ya'll used to call shack jobs. That the owner was so greedy, he made clerks give shack jobs a cheap rate since they wouldn't stay the entire night, made people go make the beds and re-rent the rooms and that sometimes the occupancy rate was over a hundred percent."

"I do recall that and recall how disgusted I was at it. Every time my wife and I go to a motel, we check the linens very carefully to make sure they're clean. Of course, back then, there wasn't that much of a selection."

"That is scary. I don't think they do that anymore."

"Well, that's definitely a good thing."

"It was nice to meet you, Max. I hope you'll come by again. Kathy will sure be sorry she missed you."

"Tell her I said hey."

"I will."

As I drove back to Pavo, I thought I should go ahead and get packed for the trip back to Nashville the next day after church and lunch at my parents.

I slid in a CD by Joe South, a Georgia native who I had become familiar with in a college music class and who had a few number one hit songs. His lyrics had been philosophical and actually very religious at some level, and as the upbeat song "Walk a Mile in My Shoes" played, I thought of Effie. She had seen life as simple, in parables, and she had a way of getting right to the truth. A lot of her wisdom, it seemed to me, came from observation and thinking, as many blacks her age were forced to do, instead of talking.

Though I grew up in a time when schools, stores, hospitals, and so forth were integrated, I had seen racism and felt the undercurrent of racism, mainly, and ironically, in the church, the one place one would imagine it would never exist, and yet, Christian churches had fueled racism early on in American history by using biblical scriptures, such as Noah's son, Ham, and Adam and Eve's son, Cain, and their being marked, as justification for God's opposition to the black race. I had not heard this in church and learned this in college and had been shocked. And immediately, as the English professor lectured on this, I recalled an incident I'd experienced in church.

It seems children are often more wise than are given credit because they see the world through honest lenses until we educate the honesty out of them. At twelve, I usually sat on the back row with my friends while we wrote notes on church bulletins.

One Sunday, I stopped in the middle of a sentence because an elderly black woman, dressed in a beautiful paisley dress and hat, walked in and hobbled down the aisle and planted herself on the front row, as the pianist was playing the prelude. I had never thought about the church being segregated before, but I realized this was the first time any black person had ever come to our church. I remember feeling good about it, and I looked around to see people leaning and whispering, and I watched the minister who was red in the face while one of the deacons, an elderly jeweler in town, walked over and whispered something in his ear. The minister then heaved himself up and walked over to the elderly woman, bent, and whispered in her ear. She promptly stood and hobbled back up the aisle and out the door.

For some reason, I felt awful. I did not know what was said, but speculated she had been asked to leave, perhaps in a disguised way, maybe by him telling her where the blacks attended church and where it was located, and I walked out the front door to see where she had gone. I saw no sign of her and wondered if she had not been real, but an angel come to check up on the Christianity in our church. I had asked for-giveness for not taking a stand because, even at twelve I knew, and realized it was people like Effie, the silent and wise ones who had in some way guided others to see life from a different perspective. I knew people like that were the true heroes in life, not politicians, actors, or millionaire suc-cess stories, selling themselves on infomercials.

As I pulled the Jeep into the driveway, it struck me odd I had made the drive back to Aunt Ophelia's without really concentrating on where I was going. It was as though the Jeep was on automatic pilot and knew exactly the way home. When I cut the engine, I just sat, staring at Aunt Ophelia's house, remembering the good times I had experienced there as a child. I would definitely miss Aunt Ophelia, and part of me felt wispy, and felt tears mist my eyes. I had not cried when I had learned of her death, and I could hear her in my memory, saying "Ain't no use in crying, praise God."

I turned my attention to checking the online newspaper in Tallahassee to see if the hotel management position was advertised and also checking to see if the job was advertised on the company's website. Tallahassee was a beautiful city, and I felt Jaden and I could live there, being close enough to our parents to assist with care and visiting on the weekend and staying at Aunt Ophelia's house, but not so close rela-tives would stop by without calling. I also needed to pack, so I began to get mentally organized and remembered I needed to charge my cell phone.

Chapter
8

After checking the hotel web site in Tallahassee, I was excited about the position. It seemed a natural fit for me, requiring three years of hotel management experience, a Bachelor's degree, and computer knowledge and skills. The Apalachee Hotel was a famous historical site. A former Spanish mission, remodeled and expanded with white stucco and clay roof tiles, the hotel sat on several acres in downtown Tallahassee near the capitol building and had been a temporary residence to actors, governors, presidents, and other politicians. The most famous were Al Gore and his team, and George W. Bush and his team, during the squabble over twenty-six electoral votes in the 2000 Presidential election. The Apalachee, too, had been the temporary hospital home to the sick and dying during the flu epidemic after World War I when then President Theodore Roosevelt had visited.

The manager of the Apalachee's salary wasn't advertised, but I wasn't too worried about that. I also checked the Tallahassee newspaper, but didn't see the ad there, and planned to check my industry magazine when I arrived back in Nashville Sunday night. I had briefly talked with Jaden, who really didn't have much to say, except she was ready for me to get home and hadn't been feeling well, which alarmed me as she never seemed to feel poorly. She alleviated my concerns be telling me it was just simple nausea and Pepto-Bismol had quelled the feelings. I packed everything before going to bed, so I could leave as soon as possible after church for the long drive back home, and I slept soundly, being awakened early by the screaming peacocks in the woods.

That morning, I had an oatmeal bar, some coffee, and I shaved and showered. I decided not to wear a tie to church and instead put on my navy blazer over a polo shirt and khakis. I slid my feet into my loafers, which needed polishing after the dust and pollen had come to rest on them. I drove over to Mama and Daddy's, but they had already gone to the church for Sunday school, which I should have remembered. When I pulled into the church parking lot, I couldn't find a space, so I parked at the post office across the street near Doug's car and walked.

I recalled the old black woman, who I assumed had been asked to leave church all those years ago, and actually looked around for her, but, of course, I didn't see her, and part of me felt crazy for having thought and acted on that instinct.

When I walked in, I didn't see Mama and Daddy in the sanctuary, but people noticed me and waved or either came up to me and said hello. It was always a good feeling, seeing people again. Out of the corner of my eye, I saw Doug sitting near the front, and then I saw Mama and Daddy come in from the side door that opened to the fellowship hall and class-rooms, and I waved at them and smiled. They smiled back and Daddy nodded. Mama never waved her hands in the air unless she was shooing away flies or mosquitoes.

Mama and Daddy always sat in the third row from the front, so I moved that way to sit with them. I was surprised Doug was already sitting there and wondered if he remembered where they sat from all those years ago when he was a regular. As I was making my way down the side aisle next to the stained-glass windows, I saw Colt and Tiffany.

Colt and Tiffany were an item in high school and we had been good friends all through school. We had gone to church together, were baptized together, in youth activities together, including 4-H camp at Rock Eagle.

The time spent at Rock Eagle was a changing one for all of us, not because of what 4-H taught us, but because of the trouble we got into. President Jimmy Carter's niece was our camp counselor, and Colt, most of the boys in our cabin, and me, snuck into the girls' cabin way after midnight, and stole their clothes, tossing them into the shallows of the lake. We had already been warned by Ms. Carter about our behavior because we had tied one boy to the bed and stuffed dirty streaked underwear over his mouth and nose. The next morning, there were screams and Ms. Carter sprinted to their cabin. We all sat by the window, peering through the blinds and hoping not to be seen. When she entered, there was silence, and in a minute, she was back out and walking our way. One boy, always scared, confessed, and we were marched to the lake, where we spent most of the morning getting wet clothes, washing them, and drying them. It was a first lesson in doing laundry for us, and the head of 4-H in Atlanta made a special trip to lecture us, told us he'd called our parents, and threatened to send us home. They didn't send us home, and Mama and Daddy never said anything about him calling, and of course, I didn't mention it.

I looked to my right and noticed other friends from childhood, Mark and Farrah. Farrah had been a beautiful girl, and though I never had gone out with her as a teen, I had thought about it. Her family was a bit more upper crust than mine had been, though it would be what Mama would call, "new money."

Once when I was about fourteen, I saw Farrah come into church in a tight sundress and sandals. She sat one row in front of me, and when we stood to sing the first hymn, I began staring at her body, her shapely bottom and her budding breasts. I couldn't keep my fantasies off her body and began to feel the sensation young males often feel. I knew I had become enlarged, spurred by my lust, and when the music minister said stand to sing "Rock of Ages," I crossed my legs and remained seated.

I knew I was blushing when Mama and Daddy turned to give me a look and I whispered "My leg is asleep." Farrah, too, turned back, looked at me, glanced toward my pants, smiled and turned around. I think it may have been the first time I seriously thought I should run away, but I learned that one must confront fear, no matter the feat. However, I did figure that incidents such as this, combined with my imagining chandeliers falling out of the ceiling and killing people I didn't like, were all being added in a column of sins that would one day be held against me.

Mark, too, had come from a "new money" family and had all the boy toys—the motorcycle, the four-wheeler, the guns. He had become an avid hog hunter at an early age, keeping expensive hunting dogs and traveling the South Georgia woods in search of wild hogs.

Once, when he was sliced down his arm by the tusks of a hog as he slit the throat, he had lost a lot of blood in the woods, but found super glue and glued the six inch long cut, stopping the bleeding. It was a story that circulated for some time, and people would still occasionally tell it.

I sat on the end of the pew, and Mama leaned over and whispered, "You need to move. My stomach is upset and I might need to leave."

"You sick?" I whispered back.

"No, it's them fried green tomatoes. They've been doing me this way for years. Takes about two days to get them out of my system."

"Oh," I said, getting up and moving over to her other side between her and Doug, in case she needed to get up in the middle of the service. I wondered why she didn't quit eating the tomatoes if they bothered her . It was also something I didn't really want to know about. Bodily functions described in such graphic detail were always the topic of conversation at Sampson's breakfast table at the hotel, where model citizens met to discuss weather, politics, and world events on a daily basis. Weather and events were how their breakfast meetings began, yet sooner or later, the conversations turned to hemorrhoids, acid reflux, corns and gout, diarrhea, problems urinating, erectile dysfunction, and so forth. Given the medical commercials that dominated television, these previously unspoken issues were now blasting across the airways, so even elementary school children knew symptoms and alleged cures, according to Jaden. I felt sure that as time marched on, I, too, might describe these in some nursing home one day, but I certainly hoped not. In earlier years, I didn't recall older relatives describing these conditions in such graphic detail, but modern society had become so desensitized, and while I did feel on certain subjects, maybe spousal or child abuse and other such topics, there needed to be open discussion, I also believed that some things are simply better left unsaid. I, for one, did not want to know about the private lives, especially sex lives, of my older family members, but for that matter, it wasn't age-related. I didn't want to know about anyone's private life. I also felt that's why they called it private, so it wouldn't be opened for the world to know. It was times like those I wanted to be a hermit.

As the prelude began with "Brethren We Have Met To Worship," the pianist hammered away at the keys, and the choir came in dressed in their robes that just a few days ago many had worn to Aunt Ophelia's service. I stared at the "This Do In Remembrance of Me" table where Aunt Ophelia's casket had been, and now the flowers on the table were in her memory. When Ms. Peggy stopped playing, the preacher stood, walked toward the podium and asked everyone to pray.

After the prayer, the preacher stood silent, gazing out over the congregation and rather than making the announcements and welcoming visitors, he said, "Today, I would like to begin by asking for your forgiveness."

Mama's elbow jammed into my rib cage, as she whispered, "Tell your daddy I told him so." I just shook my head. I wasn't going to make Doug lean over, so I could tell Daddy anything.

"I need to ask for forgiveness for all of the terrible thoughts I have had this week about many of you in the congregation who have been spreading rumors about me." There was a pause, and I was stunned.

He continued, "I have also been asked by the deacons to resign due to those clouds surrounding me, so they said. I will not address the rumors one way or another. We are all sinners in the eyes of God, and being a Christian does not excuse you from sin, whether real or imagined. One only need to recall our former President Jimmy Carter who lusted in his heart. I say who among you without sin may cast the first stone at me. I am here to tell you that after careful consideration and much prayer, I have decided that I will not resign. If this house of sinners wants me out, then cast me out." He turned, walked back to his chair, and sat.

The song director stood and tripped his way to the podium where he stuttered which page to turn in the hymn book. He didn't even motion the congregation to stand, and the song "Pass Me Not" began slow because the pianist was so shaken she began in C sharp chord instead of B flat. There was a lot of shifting, crossing legs, and whispering, and a few people got up and walked out.

I suppose if there were any visitors, it would've been a one-time visit, because it was something I had never before encountered in church. I looked across the aisle at Mrs. Mason, who sat motionless and stared blankly into space, and I glanced to my left to see Mrs. Yates, who sat and stared at the floor with her face all flushed. Daddy seemed furious, though he never showed much emotion, but I could tell by his twitching eyelid, and Mama's mouth was partially open.

I whispered, "Are you okay?"

She responded, "If I go to the bathroom now, people will think I'm reacting to the preacher. I'll just have to hold it in."

"Pass Me Not" was first followed by "Love Lifted Me" at which point I got another elbow and Mama whispered, "I'll bet it did."

The ushers took up an offering, which I would guess would have been low given the tone set by Rev. Mason, except for those like Mama and Daddy who made their checks out in advance before going to church, and the congregation stood and sang the "Doxoloy."

The preacher returned to the podium and read from Matthew 18:9, "And if your eye causes you to sin, pluck it out and cast it from you. It is better for you to enter into life with one eye, rather than having two eyes, to be cast into hell fire."

Privately, while I generally understood what was intended by a verse, I felt that particular one was stupid.

He went on to say that what you see is not what you get, contrary to what comedian Flip Wilson had been known to say back in the day. That interpretation of something we see is where the danger of hell becomes real. He told the story of a boy in his school and a teacher who thought the boy had been cheating because she'd seen the boy turn his head. She had kept him after class, accused him of cheating, and failed him. The principal had done nothing when the parents and the child complained, and the child, and his parents, had lost faith and had become disgusted with the education system. The boy's life was forever changed by the judgment that had been dished out to him. He dropped out of high school, and took a manufacturing job, like his parents, and had died early from alcohol.

Rev. Mason raised his voice. "Could this accusation have been his turning point? Could he have become an educator, a prosperous member of the community and church, or President of the United States?" He continued, "He could have, perhaps, if someone hadn't destroyed his life so early. Yes, he could've changed. Many of us changed over the years. Doug's here and he's had a conversion experience. Yes, he could've gotten over the evil done to him. We all do, but we don't ever forget. The wounds and scars are often too deep, and they're there to remind us, to warn us not to go back."

Part of me wondered about his words, and he seemed to be, at least on one level of preaching victimization, which we see so much of in society. Everyone's a victim in one sense of life and death. The point, to me, is not in relishing in your own negative experience, but taking something positive from it and moving on. The preacher wiped sweat beads from his forehead, and as he turned his head from one side of the audience to the other, the sagging skin underneath his chin shook and reminded me of a turkey gobbler neck.

Rev. Mason then read from Acts 26:18, which was about turning from darkness to light, turning from the power of Satan to God, and receiving forgiveness of sins. He finally ended with Jesus' words as he was crucified on the cross in Luke 23:34. "Father, forgive them, for they know not what they do."

It was clear to me he felt those who had gossiped about him and Mrs. Yates had turned their focus to sin by spreading rumors, and that even the negative thoughts they'd had were turning them away from the light, the truth, and going the way of evil. It was not clear to me whether he had sinned or not, but he obviously felt those who had gossiped about him had wronged him in some way.

Mama leaned over and whispered, "I feel like I've just been crucified."

I wondered if she felt guilty for mentioning the gossip, for in the preacher's eyes, mentioning it alone was a sin.

Instead of coming down front of the "This Do In Remembrance Of Me" table for the invitation, he went back to his chair and sat down. The song director, clearly flustered, came back to the pulpit and asked everyone to turn to page two hundred forty in the hymnal to sing "Just As I Am." Rather than singing all six verses, we stopped after two, and the church service ended with the song director calling on my Daddy, the head deacon, to dismiss with prayer. I had heard my Daddy pray, and usually they were positive and a little long-winded. This one, however, was abrupt. My thoughts, he was shaken, were confirmed.

The preacher stopped to talk to some of the congregation who had come up to him afterward and didn't go into the vestibule to shake hands as people exited the building. Mama and Daddy bolted for the door, but not before Daddy stopped several other deacons and whispered. I figured the preacher's sermon had done nothing, except pour gas on embers. Personally, I was ready to get in my Jeep and head back to Tennessee, and though I supposed sermons such as this often became personal, it was different in a large church, like the one

Jaden and I attended in downtown Nashville, where seventy-five percent of the people attending we didn't even know, and if there had been a personal sermon aimed at particular individuals, we wouldn't have known it.

The congregation in Pavo, however, was small, and everyone knew everything about everything going on, and it was clear to me, as one who was really not a part of this church or community, the preacher had preached about sin and forgiveness, but he had clearly not forgiven those who he had perceived had sinned against him and Mrs. Yates. If he had forgiven those who he felt had gossiped about them, then he would've come to the front to receive them, and he would've gone to the vestibule to shake their hands, and the whole incident would have been forgiven. By accusing and then backing off, he had done exactly what those he had accused had done, and I didn't see him as better or practicing what he preached.

Doug and I walked out together, and I waited until we were closer to our vehicles, and none of the church members were around to overhear. "You coming over to Mama and Daddy's for lunch?"

"Sure, that sounds good."

"What did you think of church today?"

"I thought it was great," Doug said.

"Because he mentioned your conversion?"

"No, not really, but I appreciated him mentioning that. It helps."

"You didn't think he was being hypocritical, accusing those who had been gossiping about him and Mrs. Yates and then not going down front to accept them and forgive them?"

"No, not really. If people've been doing that, then it seems they need to feel guilty for their sins."

"Okay, well, I'll meet you over there."

"Okay. See you in a minute."

When Doug and I pulled in Mama and Daddy's driveway, we parked off the cement drive in the yard between the slash pines. We stood outside and talked for a few minutes about how he was feeling. I invited him to come to Nashville to visit me and Jaden and he said he might just take me up on the offer, that he'd seen some Christian concerts advertised online in Nashville that he would like to attend. Jaden and I hadn't been to many Christian concerts, although we had been to see Amy Grant before she married Vince Gill, who I had actually met at a golf tournament.

When Mama and Daddy pulled in the driveway, they both got out and seemed exhausted.

"Ya'll come on in and eat," Daddy told us.

"I've got to go to the bathroom," Mama said, "but lunch is ready."

Mama had cooked a ham, macaroni and cheese, field peas, and biscuits. For dessert, she had baked pecan pie, and I knew I would overeat and have a hard time driving back to Nashville in the baking sun. Doug, Daddy, and I scooped food onto our plastic plates and warmed them in the micro-wave. We poured tea in plastic cups, and Daddy fixed Mama a plate. When we got the silverware and napkins, we sat down and Mama came waltzing through the kitchen in her nightgown and robe.

"You fix me a plate?"

"Sure did," Daddy told her.

She sat down, and Daddy said grace, short and sweet, and we began eating.

"Mama, this is good," I said.

"Sure is," Doug echoed.

"Well, it's nothing. Doug, you feeling all right?"

"Yes ma'am," he replied.

"Well, I couldn't believe what happened in church to-day," Mama said, adding, "what're the deacons going to do?"

"We've got a meeting this afternoon at two," Daddy revealed. "We'll have to review the church constitution, but my guess is Mason's leaving or staying will be called to a vote at a special meeting Wednesday night."

"Why do ya'll want him to leave? He seems like a good fellow. He came to see me in the hospital and has called me since I've been out. He even invited me over to his house to eat supper tonight with him and Mrs. Mason," said Doug.

"Nobody's saying he's not a good fellow, deep down, but these rumors of him and Mrs. Yates push the limit, and some of the rumors have been substantiated with evidence. Sometimes, it's best just to move on, and we thought he would, but now he's refusing. I think if he owns up to his sins, then he's gotta face his wife and my guess is he don't want to do that."

"She's liable to put a bullet in him just like Mrs. Yates did her husband," supplied Mama.

"Probably not," Daddy returned. "I don't think she's the violent type."

"I don't either," Mama agreed. "But sometimes, people snap. Looks like she's about half-snapped now just with the rumors."

"I just hate the whole situation," I put in. "Hate that ya'll have to go through this, hate that he's making everyone go through it. I found it interesting he didn't even come down front for the invitation or go to the vestibule to shake hands. Whether he's guilty or not, he preached to ya'll about sin, but he ain't practicing what he preaches when it comes to for-giveness."

"Don't matter none," Mama voiced her opinion. "We'll put him out next week. Then we'll see what he does with Mrs. Yates or his wife. My bet is he won't give up his wife for Mrs. Yates. I don't know how he feels. Don't want to know, but I do know he's gotta wonder about that gun of Mrs. Yates. Police didn't take it from her, saying a woman living alone in the country needs some protection, but I'd say no one in their right mind would go out there and mess with her after what she did."

"That seems awfully cruel," Doug said.

Mama's nostrils flared and she inhaled and exhaled deeply, squinted her eyes, and reached her hand to Doug's. "Doug, it's not cruel, but a church is run by its people, the majority of which ain't gonna put up with this nonsense. You're entitled to have your say, too, regardless of what it is, but you got to remember that you ain't been involved in the church in a long time. We're glad you are and hope you'll continue to be, but something like this is better left to the deacons to handle since they are more informed."

Doug nodded, and Daddy didn't say anything. The conversation shifted to Mama's pecan pie, and though I wanted an additional piece, I decided I should probably avoid it. I helped clear the table by scraping what few remains were on the plastic plates into the trash can and rinsing the plates off in the sink. One thing I had noticed over the years is that Mama and Daddy reuse just about everything they can, including plastic plates, cups, and tin foil. It's part of their generation's behavior, having been raised by parents who had to live through the depression.

Chapter
9

After we cleaned up and I rested about thirty minutes, I told Mama, Daddy, and Doug, I really needed to get on the road and that Jaden hadn't been feeling well and I wanted to get home to her. They were all concerned, naturally, but I assured them it was probably just allergies. The pine pollen had been the major allergen to us when we lived in Georgia, but once we moved to Tennessee, we learned the major metropolitan cities of Tennessee—Nashville, Knoxville, Memphis and Chattanooga—were in the top worst places to live for sufferers of allergies. Interestingly, though, it wasn't the pine pollen, but a plethora of pollens from other trees, and after all, middle Tennessee, specifically McMinnville, was known as the nursery capitol of the world.

Doug and I shook hands, and I hugged Mama and Daddy. Daddy told me to think about moving home. I told him I would, but I didn't want to get into a drawn-out conversation about the Apalachee, Tallahassee, Aunt Ophelia's house, or anything else. I told them I'd call them Wednesday night to see how the church meeting had gone. I told Doug to give me a call and that he was welcome to come stay at our condo whenever he wanted, we'd go to a concert with him, and might even set him up with one of Jaden's school-teacher friends. He laughed. They told me to be careful as I got in the

Jeep. I drove out of Pavo and turned onto Highway 122, which would lead me past Jaden's family farm of peach orchards that smell like sweet perfume in the spring. I traveled through the town of Barney and onto Interstate 75 at Hahira, a cute town not much different than Pavo which Ray Stephens made famous in a couple of his humorous songs.

As I turned on the Interstate, the only thing that kept popping into consciousness was the fact that I had eight hours driving time, and I was exhausted already. The good lunch didn't help because every time I had a huge meal, I just wanted to take a nap. Those feelings combined with the clickety-clack of the Jeep tires hitting the creases in the pavement on the Interstate formed a repetitive sound that made me drowsy.

Near Adel and Sparks, I smiled, remembering what my Daddy told me many years ago. He had relatives who lived in Adel, and he said Adel was so close to hell, that one could see sparks. The concrete barriers that had been placed so close to the edge of the Interstate caused me to focus on driving more. The tractor-trailers seem to speed, even when the signs clearly warned them to stay in the right-hand lane and drive slower due to the lack of a shoulder. I never saw tractor-trailers pulled over and receiving tickets, but I did notice plenty of other vehicles pulled over all along the highway, getting tickets for going faster than the speed limit allowed. I didn't drive fast, but I wasn't a slow poke either. I tried to drive defensively, watching the other vehicles, and fortunately, I hadn't had an accident since my first date with Kathy.

Outside Tifton, known to be one of the most beautiful small towns in Georgia and home to the Agrirama, a living history center that exhibited life as it had been in the late 1800's with a logging train, grist mill, blacksmith shop, stores, one-room schoolhouse, and an abundance of demonstrated activities from farming to quilt-making, I noticed several wreaths on the side of the road, where the bark was missing from a pine tree. Obviously, someone had been killed there, running off the road and having a head-on collision with a long leaf pine. I felt sorry for the person, for their family, and I wondered if that person had been drunk or on drugs. I was paying attention to the memorial and almost ran into the concrete barrier, and thought these memorials, while clearly being a positive move for families during the grieving process, might actually cause others to lose focus and wreck themselves, which was the primary reason I hadn't put up a wreath and memorial for Aunt Ophelia.

I thought about Aunt Ophelia and the letter I found and wondered what other family secrets I might not know about. I thought about genetics and worried about any future children Jaden and I might have. I thought about the church incident and how this affected my parents. I wondered if the preacher did have an affair with Mrs. Yates, and how the Yates' children were handling the death of their father. Even though he had apparently been an abusive man, he was still their father. I wondered how people dealt with such situations. I counted myself fortunate not to have experienced such a life. I thought about my visit to the Thomasville Grill and my conversation with Effie. I wondered if it was fate that I learned of the job at the Apalachee from Effie and speculated if I would have learned of it had I not spontaneously stopped by for lunch. I contemplated Doug's situation, his having been in detox at the hospital and his conversion experience, and wondered if it would take hold and keep him on the straight and narrow.

Once these had run through my mind, I was near Macon and needed gas. I stopped just off the bypass at a gas station, filled the Jeep, grabbed a caffeine-free diet Coke, and headed out again. Around Forsyth, the northbound Interstate lanes expanded from two to four, so heavy traffic for a Sunday afternoon felt like much less. I visualized how traffic in Atlanta would be, how I hoped it would be.

There were not many times, if any, over the years when I had gone back and forth from Nashville to Pavo that Atlanta traffic was light. With several Interstates meeting and departing in downtown Atlanta, it was often a nightmare. What bothered me most were that Atlantians seemed to drive twenty to thirty miles over the speed limit, regardless of the amount of traffic. Once when Jaden and I were coming back from Pavo, we got stuck in Atlanta because someone was hanging on the edge of an overpass, threatening to plummet into traffic and commit suicide. A few moments didn't seem to matter much to us. We had become in engaged in a conversation that at the time seemed important. After thirty minutes of being stuck, we had become annoyed, and I made the comment that I wished he would either fall or be rescued—anything but just sitting in traffic, wasting time.

We pulled off and had lunch at a Chick-Fil-A. I remember it well because it was shortly after we'd been married and one of the first arguments we'd had about the subject of food. Jaden ordered the grilled chicken salad, and I ordered the twelve nugget meal, which included waffle fries, cole slaw, and a large drink. At that time, I wasn't off caffeine, so I drank a regular Coke. I also enjoyed dipping my nuggets and waffle fries in honey mustard sauce.

Jaden was quiet for a while, and then asked, "Is yours good?"

"Sure is," I responded, at which point she began to lecture me about my arteries. When we'd finished striking at each other in tone and without raising our voices, we left and didn't say much for some time. The radio announced that the poor guy who had been hanging from a bridge over the Interstate had given in to the police and counselors on the scene and agreed to go for treatment. In the process of being rescued, he slipped and plummeted onto the Interstate below him, where a helicopter had to land to life flight him to Emory University Hospital to be treated for several broken bones and several internal injuries.

I never knew if the poor fellow lived or died, and I thought it was ironic how journalists failed to follow up on many stories that made the headlines. They seemed to focus their reports on the negative outcomes and forget any positive ones. It made the news even more disgusting to watch than it actually was.

Once past Kennesaw, I began to see small mountains I had become so familiar with living in Tennessee. They were majestic and beautiful, and I could certainly understand why so many people were attracted to these areas, especially the most popular park in the world—the Great Smokey Mountain National Forest.

One weekend a few years ago, Jaden and I had gone to visit the Smokies, and we toured Cades Cove. It was the most beautiful little village sandwiched between the mountains I had ever seen, and I had even wanted to move there. Jaden said I was nuts, but it had made a major impression on me. Aside from the beautiful churches, cabins, and cantilever barns, wildlife was abundant and roamed openly. One could easily see turkey, deer, and bears. What I got from my trip to Cades Cove was a crystal Christmas ornament, which I'd hang proudly on the tree each year.

Once we'd left Cades Cove, we drove Newfound Gap's road, the only connector between Gatlinburg, Tennessee, and Cherokee, North Carolina. This road leads to Clingman's Dome, the highest point in Tennessee. Never before had I been to places so high, and not having grown up in the mountains, I felt some anxiety, especially as we drove the narrow road with no guardrail and drop-offs of about five thousand feet. I'd imagined being shoved off the road by senior citizens in a huge motor home they had not been trained to drive. Fortunately, that didn't happen, but going down the mountains and arriving in Cherokee made me feel a great deal better. Cherokee was an impressive town with its natural history displays and shows. I couldn't help but think what natives have had to go through over the years and hoped my ancestors hadn't played any role in their demise. It was said one of my great-great grandmothers was part Creek Indian, and the dark hair and olive complexion had come to us from her. There was no proof of this, of course, since natives only had oral history. I was thankful, though, that our trip plans had us going in a different direction that would avoid the roller-coaster mountain road prior to going back to our condo in Nashville.

The lunch had settled by the time I got to Dalton, so I stopped for a cup of coffee. I felt like coffee might perk me up for the rest of the trip, or at least the taste and smell would make me think so, since I would get decaf. The Starbucks was swamped with customers, but I finally got a decaf latte. I found a small leather wingback chair by the window and plopped down to relax and slowly sip the coffee. The drive had felt difficult, and I could feel the tenseness in my back and neck muscles. I saw a white BMW convertible pull in, and watched the blonde bombshell step out and walk toward Starbucks. As I watched, I recalled the story from the preacher of Jimmy Carter lusting in his heart, and it occurred to me that most men, and probably most women, couldn't help but look and lust. It seemed almost natural for a human being to do so, and seeing the blonde reminded me of one of the most interesting times in the history of Jaden and me. We had split up briefly in college, stemming from an argument about getting married and moving away from South Georgia. My friends had urged me to go out on a date to make Jaden jealous, and some of them told me to call Suzanne, a blonde who drove a convertible BMW and whose father owned part of Coca-Cola. My mind reeled with fantasies of inheriting large sums of money, living in a house in the Caribbean, and drinking Piña Coladas. They gave me her number and I jotted it down and didn't call for a couple of weeks. Finally, giving up on Jaden, I dialed the number and talked to Suzanne and we agreed to meet for lunch at a café downtown. While I sat in the café gulping sweet tea and waiting on Suzanne, Jaden breezed in the café and plopped down.

"What're you doing here, Max?" she asked.

"Getting ready to have lunch," I quickly responded.

"Alone?"

"Well, no, I was supposed to meet someone." My heart had fluttered.

"Hmmm. Bill, Terry, Steven?"

"No, a girl."

"Really? Giving up on me so quickly?"

"No, Jaden. Everyone just encouraged me to get out and meet someone."

"Well, who is she?"

"Her name is Suzanne."

"What does she look like?"

"Blonde. Don't know what else. Haven't seen her. I think she has a BMW."

"I think I know her. Does her dad own part of Coca Cola?"

"Yes, I think so. Do you know her?"

"Sure do. She's my neighbor and we're good friends. That's why she sent me here to meet you. She couldn't come. So, why don't I join you instead and let's talk?" Jaden smiled.

"Okay, sure. But you knew all this in advance, didn't you?"

"Yes, Suzanne knew there was probably only one Max around and so she came to me after you called her and told me she didn't want to get involved in our squabble. I told her I would keep the date for her."

"Well, I guess my Coca-Cola stock, BMW, and so on just went up in the air."

"That's right. It's back to a brunette, an Accord, and a peach orchard."

We both laughed and talked, and before lunch had ended, we were back to a couple. As the years had passed, and we would argue, I would tell Jaden I could have had a BMW and some Coca Cola stock, and she would tell me, "Nothing stopping you," and generally, we'd both bust out laughing.

When I got to Chattanooga, I-75 and I-24 split, and I took I-24 toward Nashville. Traffic in Chattanooga could be heavy at times, but thank goodness, this wasn't one of those times. The Interstate curved back and forth over hills and Nickajack Lake before finally climbing Monteagle Mountain. Once I was off the mountain and neared Manchester, I called Jaden on the cell to let her know where I was. I asked her if she wanted me to pick up anything for dinner and she said that even though she still felt somewhat nauseous, she wanted some fried chicken. I thought the last thing she needed was something fried if she was nauseous and I almost told her, having remembered our argument over my arteries, but after a second thought, I decided to keep my mouth shut. Some-times in a marriage, it's better just to let things go, not to bring more attention to them. All it does is cause trouble, stick in memory and resurface from time to time. That it does so naturally seems to indicate it's trying to tell folks to get rid of it somehow, but many don't, and I imagine that's part of the trouble in relationships.

Traffic picked up around Murfreesboro, where there was a lot of construction and got even heavier the closer I got to Nashville as Interstates 24, 40, and 65 all merged. I turned off the Fourth Avenue exit and went through the drive-thru at Kentucky Fried Chicken and ordered two chicken breast meals.

Once I turned into the gated entrance, slid my card into the security gadget, the gate opened, and I pushed the garage door opener, the door slid up, I pulled the Jeep in, and turned off the ignition. I climbed out, taking the KFC bag and stretched a bit to alleviate the stiffness. I looked around at Nashville, and nothing seemed different. The BellSouth Tower, which everyone called the Bat Tower because it looked like something architecturally out of Gotham City, the L&M building, the Cumberland River Bridge, and the slow moving river with a barge.

Jaden opened the laundry room door in the garage and said hey. I walked up to her, gave her a kiss, and handed her the KFC bag. I told her I needed to get the peaches and that I would be right in. I closed the garage and lugged the box of peaches up the stairs and into the kitchen. The garage and laundry room were the only parts of our condo on the first floor. Every other room was upstairs. We fixed our plates and sat on the balcony.

"I sure am glad you're home."

"Me, too."

"Max, I need to tell you something."

"What is it? Something wrong?"

"I didn't tell you because you would worry, but when I was sitting out here the other night, really late because I couldn't sleep, I saw two men assault a woman and throw her in the river."

"Oh my God, Jaden. Did you call the police?"

"Yes, I did. It was on the news the next morning that the woman was homeless, and I believe these two guys were drunk."

"Were they homeless, too?"

"No, they were downtown partying. They weren't from Nashville."

"Did you have to go downtown to identify them?"

"No, the security cameras at the Hard Rock Café recorded them, but I had to see the film and sign a statement saying it was them. I may have to go to court, and I don't mind doing that, but what they did to her by slinging her off into the river was horrific, and I was in a state of shock. I couldn't believe someone would do that, and I feel so guilty for not having yelled at them or something. I didn't even think about yelling until after she was swallowed up, and even then, I wanted to yell, but couldn't for fear they'd come here and kill me, too. The police caught them downtown that same night because they went right back to partying. They didn't find the woman's body until the next day, and there was an interview on TV with her mother who lives here in town. They'd had a fight and she'd moved out of her mother's house and took to living on the streets. It's just all so sad. I want to do something for her mother." Jaden wiped tears from her eyes.

"We'll do something, and that's just the craziest thing I ever heard. You think you'll have to go to court? I would fear some of their friends or family might do something."

"The district attorney says probably not. It really depends on whether their attorneys want to put me on the stand. The two guys did confess, hoping for a lighter sentence."

"Lighter sentence for telling the truth?"

"It does seem somehow disgusting, doesn't it?"

"Yes, it does. Jaden, I'm sorry. You gonna be all right?"

"I think so."

"Is that why you've been nauseous?"

"Maybe, but I really don't think so. I was nauseous before that happened. I probably ought to go to the doctor. I think it's sinus drainage. If nothing else, maybe I can get something to help me sleep more at night. With you being gone, and with witnessing that murder, I have had a very difficult few days. It's hard for me to sit out here and look at that river now. I wonder how many others are in that river who were never found."

"Who knows?"

"I just don't understand how someone can do that at all. I mean, I can't imagine killing anyone even in self defense, like that Ms. Yates, which I don't recall you telling me about."

"I didn't tell you about that, did I? I must've forgotten. Sorry. Meghan and I were pretty good friends, and I used to go over there, but it was creepy the way their dad looked at me."

"You think he did something to his own kids?"

"No, Meghan never indicated that, and I didn't get that sense. But I could tell there was some abuse there. Well, Mrs. Yates shot him in the privates, let him suffer a while, and then finally finished him off. See, I can't even imagine that, and I guess that's more like self defense, even though it's not like an intruder."

"Yeah, I don't know. Murder's murder though, and I don't know what was going on with them guys and that homeless woman, but I just don't think it was worth being killed that way. I started to go down there to the river when I saw the police and the rescue people, but I just couldn't bear the thought of her being dead just like that."

"Maybe those guys didn't think they had killed her by throwing her in the river."

"I'm sure they didn't ask her if she could swim first."

"No, probably not. When the police caught them, did they say what happened?"

"One news report said they thought she was a prostitute and wouldn't do business with them and they got mad."

"So they slung her into the river? That's just nuts."

"Yes, it is."

While I knew Jaden would never forget what she saw, and this would probably haunt her the rest of her life, as it would've me had I seen it, I didn't know what else to say. I felt really bad for her, and I just made an internal vow that I would be there for her as she needed me, too.

Jaden and I ate our chicken and she cleaned up while I unloaded my Jeep. There was laundry that needed to be done, and I wanted to get a good night's sleep, but I felt I needed to tell Jaden about the possible job at the Apalachee. I was really too tired. I didn't know how she'd take it and certainly didn't want to make her feel any more sick than she already felt, but at the same time, I knew if I didn't tell her, she'd be mad. I did call Mama and Daddy and let them know I had made it home okay. I told them I'd call them Wednesday to find out about the church meeting.

Once Jaden and I were in bed, I told her about the church meeting, and she was surprised. "That's just awful," she said. "I guess I ought to call my parents, too, but they aren't all that active, and I doubt they'll go."

"Jaden, I need to tell you something, too. I read an email when I was in Georgia from Mr. Sampson. He's hired a new vice president. I was mad as hell that he didn't promote me, and I haven't talked to him, but I feel like I've been betrayed somehow. What tops this off is the guy he hired worked for Kovacs, that sleazy developer from Rotary and has never worked in the hotel industry. What all this means is that I assume I'll be reporting to the new guy. I'm not very happy at all, and of course, your parents and mine want us to move back and live in Aunt Ophelia's house. I noticed a job as manager of the Apalachee Hotel in Tallahassee and thought I might apply. We could live there, you could easily get a job there, and we'd be a lot closer to our parents. We could even stay at Aunt Ophelia's house on the weekend. What do you think?"

"I'm really too tired to think, Max, but it seems to me that Sampson must've had a reason for doing what he did. It may not be a reason you like, but if you feel it's time to move on, let's just do it. If it's meant to be, it will. I would like to live closer to my parents, you know that. I never really wanted to leave, but I did because I married you. I never resented it, and we've grown a lot and learned a lot, but some-times, it's just time to go. Sampson may not want to fire you or let you go, but you just need to chalk it up to experience and appreciate the opportunities you've had. You could do more and move up and I always liked Tallahassee. Lots of places to shop in Tallahassee."

"Well, leave it up to you to make a life decision based on what stores are there."

We both laughed, and I knew she really didn't feel that way, but it took the seriousness away from the moment. I was surprised that I was so sleepy and kept yawning. I don't re-member falling asleep, but was startled when Jaden woke me.

"Max, you asleep?"

"I think I was."

"I just can't sleep for thinking about that homeless woman."

"Jaden, there was nothing you could've done. You called the police, you will corroborate what the police already know, and you will do something for the woman's mother. What more can you do?"

"I don't know. Maybe do something for the homeless."

"We can certainly do that. I'll be happy to send a check to the shelter."

"Throwing money at a problem doesn't solve the prob-lem."

"No, but it does help those problems. Why don't you take a Benadryl? That will help your drainage and help you sleep."

"All right."

Chapter
10

W hen the alarm began beeping at five o'clock in the morning, I could barely get up and walk across the room to the chest-of-drawers to turn it off. I had strategically placed it there to force me to get out of bed. I knew Jaden wouldn't. She could sleep through a tornado, and in fact, had slept right through a tornado, or what meteorologically speaking was labeled a wall cloud.

I had been at work at the hotel at the time, and guests and staff had taken cover in the basement, which was where the laundry was located. Windows from high rises downtown had been blown out, and there had been quite a bit of damage to roofs, landscaping, and phone and electrical services. Cars, too, that had not been parked in garages downtown had tons of hail damage and had broken windshields and windows. Jaden had been off that day due to a holiday and had taken a nap. When I finally got home late in the afternoon, she was still asleep and had heard nothing. Fortunately, no one had died in that tornado, but the sixty or so tornadoes that came through the state of Tennessee had wreaked havoc and killed many people in parts of West Tennessee, and it seemed sad to me that the TV reporters found the oddest people to interview.

I turned the coffee pot on, shaved, and showered, and walked back into the bedroom and told Jaden it was time to get up. She opened one eye and said, "In a minute."

I headed back to the kitchen, poured coffee, turned on the local news, and decided to go back again and wake her. She had turned over, gone back to sleep. She wasn't too thrilled the second time around either, but she did get up and shuffle to the bathroom. I began getting dressed for work, and Jaden poured coffee and watched the news, too. When I was ready to walk out the door, she got up to shower. She seemed more awake, but began to gag and ran to the trashcan in the kitchen where she dropped to her knees, hugging the can, and retched. Watching her heave made me want to throw up, too, and I felt the gag reflex tickle my throat, but I didn't. She didn't even have anything in her stomach to throw up, except drainage.

"Maybe you ought to call in and go see a doctor. Maybe they can give you something stronger than Benadryl to dry up your sinuses and stop the drainage."

She looked at me with watery eyes. "I think I will, if I can get an appointment."

"I need to go. Will you be all right?"

"Yeah, I guess."

"Okay, love you."

"Love you, too." I gave her a kiss and went out the door. I made a mental note to call her once I was at the hotel and check on her.

Traffic wasn't that heavy in downtown yet, but as I drove out of the complex parking lot, I could see the backups on I-65, which is the main reason we'd bought a condo in the downtown area, so we didn't have to get on the Interstate.

When I got to the hotel, I noticed Sampson sitting at the breakfast table in the café with his cronies. He didn't see me. I went on back to my office and was greeted by several of the staff who didn't know if I knew Kovacs' protégé, Bennett Fillmore, had been hired as the new vice president. Many said Sampson should have hired me instead and couldn't believe what had happened. Some thought I had been fired. Anytime there's a change in an organization, rumors tend to fly. I told them I appreciated their comments and felt all would be well.

I also told them everything would work out for the best, and they needed to have faith that Sampson was doing the right thing, even though I didn't personally believe it.

I caught up on email before going through regular mail. I checked my newest issue of "Hotels" and didn't see the posting for the job at the Apalachee. While that might have disturbed some, it actually made me feel good they hadn't advertised the position because there would be less competition. I stuffed the magazine in my briefcase to take home to read. I dialed Jaden, and she answered, "Hello?"

"Hey, you feeling all right?"

"I feel a little better. I did call the doctor and got an appointment after lunch at Vanderbilt."

"Good. Why don't you just rest until then?"

"I think I will, and I'll call you later on when I get back."

"Okay, be careful. Call me if you need me."

"I will," and the phone went dead.

I pulled a stack of work from my inbox on my desk that included some junk mail and some reports from the night auditors. A quick glance revealed that everything was in order, and our occupancy rate had been high the few days I'd been away. There was a light knock on the door, and I said, "Come on in."

"Hey, Max. Welcome back."

"Hey, Mr. Sampson. Thanks."

"I'm sorry about your aunt."

"I appreciate that."

"Did ya'll get the flowers?"

"Probably so. I didn't look, but I'm sure my mama did." I nearly told him about the wreath with the phone, but thought he might have sent it, so decided not to.

"Well, I suppose you read my email while you were there."

"Yes, I did."

"Mind if I sit?"

"Of course not." I thought that was strange since it was his chair, his office, his hotel.

Mr. Sampson closed the door, sat in the wingback chair

across from my desk. "I figured you'd be mad as hell when you read it, but my intention was not to make you mad."

"I wasn't mad," I lied, "but I was surprised."

"Well, Max, it's complicated, and I've been backed into a corner."

"What do you mean?"

"I had to hire Fillmore. It's a long story. Essentially, his granddaddy owns the First Nashville Bank and, of course, he went to Vanderbilt. That right there ought to tell you I ain't much in favor of him since I'm such a U.T. fan, but hell, I borrowed a lot of money a few years back from his granddaddy when I refurbished the hotel. Problem is, the land the hotel sits on is leased, and I was assured the lease was for a hundred years. Well, it was, but you know, when this hotel was first built it was leased land, and that hundred year lease was up last year. I've been trying to get them to sell me the land for months, legally getting a continuation while this was negotiated. Old man Fillmore's son, as you know, is a big-time lawyer here and very involved with politics at the capitol. Well, Bennett Fillmore's father married Eliza Bennett, daughter of former Governor Bennett, which is where he got his first name. Anyway, to make a long story short, I'm backed into a corner. They won't sell me the land. I had to lease the land, and to keep the rate low, old man Fillmore indicated his grandson had majored in management and was interested in working in hotel management, after he had worked for the developer Kovacs. He didn't tell me outright to hire him, but he indicated that the family, including former Governor Bennett, would appreciate any good word I could put in for him with some of the other hotel owners in town in case I didn't have an opening here. You know these people have a reputation for taking from the poor and giving to themselves. I'm not a poor man, Max, but I think I will be when these leeches get through with me."

"That's awful."

"I'll tell you what's awful. This Bennett Fillmore walks around here with a smirk on his face, and the staff members hate him already after only a few days. I haven't had customer complaints yet, but I know they'll come. I'm not going to make you suck up to him, Max, and I'm not going to get rid of you. You built this place for me, but sooner or later, Fillmore and Kovacs would like to see this historical hotel bulldozed for a new development, and it could happen. I could sell the hotel, and I would make some money, since it's paid off, but old man Fillmore knows that, too. He'd bid low for it because he knows he'll get it. The land lease continuance only goes for another two years. Nobody would buy it outside of a developer because of the land lease. I should have thought more about that up front, but I trusted them, and you know hindsight is twenty-twenty."

"It always is."

"You can stay as long as you want, and you'll still report to me. I'm going to put Fillmore in charge of some projects, fluff stuff, just to keep his weasel ass working. But any time you want to go, you say the word. I'll give you enough bonuses to keep you going for some time. I kind of wish, looking back, that I had given you part of the hotel stock. You know I always thought of you as my own, and I regret this more than you'll ever know."

"Don't regret it. It doesn't do any good. I appreciate everything you've done for me and always will. When I was home for my aunt's funeral, I realized that I wouldn't mind moving back to that area. Jaden has always wanted to move home, but I wasn't really interested. I heard about a manager's position in Tallahassee at the Apalachee Hotel and thought I might apply, if you don't mind."

"The Apalachee? Ha! I hadn't heard that name in years. Don't ever tell Earline this, but a girl I dated at U.T. was from Tallahassee, and her Daddy owned the Apalachee. Oh, she was a good-looking thing, Italian from what I remember. I wouldn't even mind calling down there for you."

"No, that's okay. I'll apply first. They'll probably call you for a reference."

"Not a problem at all, Max. Anything I can do. I better get to running my errands. I'll see you back around lunch, but I'll tell you one thing. I wish my parents were still here.

Nothing like loving your family while they're here. Once they're gone, there's a void."

I nodded.

"If you see Bennett slinking around the hotel, introduce yourself to him and be nice. Offer to help him, if you don't mind. I'm sure he would refuse any help."

"I'll do it."

"If you were to get that position in Tallahassee, I'd give him your responsibilities. I'd work his ass off."

We both chuckled, and Sampson was out the door. I felt like weight had been lifted from my shoulders and felt sorry for Sampson. In his twilight years, even with his intelligence and money, he had been and was going to be, taken advantage of, and I wondered about other senior citizens who were taken advantage of all for the sake of money. I'd seen scams on news reports, and while I didn't think I would ever fall victim to a scam, I think if one has any vulnerability at all, it would be easy to become prey.

At lunch, I ate in the restaurant with Sampson. Bennett had disappeared, and we speculated he'd gone to meet his father and grandfather at the City Club, which is where most of the loaded people ate. Sampson talked about his health, Earline's health, and we talked about the upcoming college football season. After lunch, I did a walk-about and inspected rooms, the kitchen, and the grounds. I had a meeting with the kitchen manager and the front desk manager, and by the end of the meetings, it was almost time to go home. I wondered if Jaden was home, but I called and didn't get an answer. I decided to leave a little early, beat the flood of traffic out of downtown. When I got home, Jaden's car was in the garage and I found her outside on the balcony in the Cracker Barrel rocking chair with her legs propped on a wicker ottoman.

"Hey, what're you doing?"

"Not much, just relaxing."

I plopped in the other rocker. "Did you miss going to school today?"

"Not really."

"How was the doctor's appointment?"

"It was all right."

"What'd they say?"

"Doctor seemed to think it was drainage like I suspected, but said I might have an infection that was making me nauseous. They took some blood and a urine sample. I should have the results in a day or two. How was your day?"

"It was good, believe it or not." I told her about Bennett Fillmore, his family and their connections, the problems with the leased land, and what Sampson had said, including that I shared with him about our need to go home and the job opening at the Apalachee.

"Well, now, at least, I feel a little better."

"Me, too. I'm going in, edit my old cover letter, and submit that and my resume in an email. Hopefully, they'll call me. They didn't advertise in the hotel magazine."

"It may be they have an internal candidate, which is why they didn't advertise nationally. Plus that costs a lot."

"I didn't think about that, but I hope that's not true."

"If it is, you'll get something sooner or later. There's no rush, really."

I went to our bedroom, where I changed clothes and booted up the computer. Once I Googled the Apalachee, I went to their site and went to the job section. Their human resources person's email was there, so I clicked and a new message box addressed to her popped up. I wrote a quick introductory note, minimized the email, opened Word, edited the cover letter, and saved it. The resume was up-to-date because we had to make certain personnel files at the hotel were in order and current for auditing purposes by the state. I attached both documents to the email and clicked "send." Within minutes, I received an auto-reply from someone in Human Resources, verifying they'd received the materials and thanking me for my interest in the Apalachee.

I walked into the den, glanced through the French doors to the balcony, and Jaden had her eyes closed, so I went to the kitchen to pour a caffeine-free diet Coke. I looked in the freezer and the refrigerator and wondered what we would eat for dinner. There didn't seem to be anything that immediately appealed to my senses, so I snacked, eating some cheese and crackers. When the phone rang, I answered on the first ring.

"Mr. Peacock?"

"Yes?"

"Is Jaden in?"

"She is, but she's resting at the moment. Can I take a message?"

"This is Lacy from Dr. Patel's office calling. We wanted to advise her not to take the allergy medication we gave her earlier this afternoon."

"Why not? Was it bad or something?"

"No, not at all. I don't know if I'm supposed to tell you this or not." She paused and my heart felt like it had stopped completely. "Jaden is pregnant. The lab confirmed this by the urine sample this afternoon. We then called the lab for blood work results, too." Another pause between both of us. "Mr. Peacock?"

"Yes, I'm here. I'll tell you what. Let me get her for you and you tell her. I don't think I can."

"Okay."

I called Jaden to the phone. She got up sluggishly, and I went to the French door, flung it open, and handed her the phone. "Who is it?" she whispered.

"The doctor's office."

"Hello?"

And, of course, I couldn't hear them, but I could hear Jaden.

"What? Pregnant? But I'm on the pill."

"I know it's not one hundred percent, but it's close."

"Okay, I won't take it. Yes, let me get a pen." She scribbled something down. "Okay, yes, I'll be there." Jaden clicked the phone off.

I began laughing. "This is great. Just in time for us to move closer to home."

Jaden started crying. "I just didn't think about being pregnant. I feel so stupid, but that explains my crazy appetite and also my nausea. You knew I hated fried chicken!"

I just laughed. "Should we call our parents?"

"No, not yet. Let's get some more info first."

"But we need to tell someone."

"No, not yet. You'll jinx it if you tell."

Jaden sometimes was overly superstitious. I didn't believe in any sort of jinx, but it was difficult for me to keep any sort of news secret. I actually got some sort of adrenaline rush from learning news no one knew. I think it went back to my high school days.

"How do you feel?"

"Well, this wasn't the planned pregnancy I'd always thought we'd have."

"No, but sometimes, life makes it that way on purpose."

I didn't want to tell Jaden that this was God's way of telling her obsessive-compulsive and overly organizational tendencies wouldn't do her any good in the long run because I thought she would slap me, and now, I had to think about a baby, not just how Jaden felt. The baby and she were one, and what affected Jaden would affect the baby.

"You're right. I'll bet I won't sleep well tonight."

"You need to. I bet you will and I won't!" We both laughed.

"You know my mind is reeling with thoughts. What the name will be, what he or she will look like, if his or her health will be good, how to decorate the room."

"Come on, Jaden, let's go to bed. There's plenty of time to think about those things later. I wonder if we can still have sex."

"Max! That's a typical male response. All these important things and you're thinking about sex!"

"Sure, why not? I was also thinking about a BMW."

"I'll bet you were. You can still have that BMW, Coca-Cola stock, and probably Suzanne, too. I heard she's been married three times. You could be the fourth."

"That's okay. I need to stick around for Max Junior."

"Forget that, buddy." Jaden looked at me seriously, and said, "You know I'm gonna get fat."

"Just your belly."

Tears formed in her eyes. "But I've never been fat."

"Well, if it makes you feel better, I can call you names now before you get fat."

"No! That's ridiculous. Now, even if you don't call me names, you'll probably be thinking it and so will everyone else."

"I promise I won't."

"You won't even have to say anything. It'll be the way you and others look at me that will make me know I'm fat."

"Face it, Jaden. You'll have to gain weight, but it won't stay there forever. Hell, not with the way you eat!"

"Maybe not."

Jaden and I changed and went to bed. She fell asleep pretty quickly, but I tossed and turned. I rubbed her back, thinking that might wake her and get her interested. I had become suddenly interested and felt it, but after no response, I turned over and thought about Aunt Ophelia and wondered if she, and others who had gone on before her, could see into the hearts of men, more specifically, my lust. I also thought about the Apalachee, worried about Sampson, wondered about Mama and Daddy and their church problem, and most of all, I thought about the unborn child. It seemed from that moment on, I didn't lose my own personal identity, but I added another one, the baby, and instead of thinking of myself, or myself and Jaden, or whatever circle of people I typically thought of—family, friends, co-workers—I now included the baby in that circle.

Chapter
11

Tuesday and Wednesday at work went fairly well, at least for all I knew, since I felt like I was in a fog, my attention focusing on our unborn child. When I would arrive at work, and people would ask me questions or there was some item or another that needed my attention, I would answer them or act, but it was like driving a long distance when the unconscious takes over and after the trip is over, you're not sure how you got to your destination.

I kept wondering if the child would be a boy or girl, what we would name him or her, what he or she would grow up to be like. I was rounding a corner on the first floor, thinking about the child and mentally debating names when I almost collided with Bennett Fillmore.

"Oh, excuse me, Bennett."

"Well, good morning. You're Max Peacock, right?"

"Yes."

Bennett was dressed in a nice suit, Brooks Brothers shirt and tie, and wing tips. His dirty blond hair was parted on the side and had a wedge cut in the back. If I'd seen him from behind, he would have reminded me of Geraldine Ferraro in a pants suit. Bennett extended his hand and we shook briefly. His handshake was limp, and I felt uncomfortable about that, having always been taught to have a firm grip and not trust someone without one.

"Good to meet you. You can call me Bennett."

I certainly wouldn't have called him Mr. Fillmore, but I could have called him a few other things. "Likewise. If you need anything, let me know."

"Actually, I would like to talk to you."

"Now?" I was a bit annoyed to be brought to the reality of having a conversation with him instead of imagining the future.

"Is this a bad time?"

"No, not at all. You want to come back to my office?"

"No, we can talk here."

"Okay." I didn't like having personal conversations in the hallway, where people might hear. Of course, if someone came down the hallway, and you stopped the conversation until he or she passed, then automatically, that person knew you were having a conversation that was more private and suited for an office.

"I need to confidentially talk to you about a few items. First, do you want to have lunch with me and some of my family at the City Club maybe next week?"

"I can probably work that out. I don't know what's on my calendar."

I did not honestly want to commit to anything, but the thought of having lunch with him was sickening enough. Add his family to it, and it would be damned near a nightmare. I could imagine them sitting there, laughing these "ha-ha" laughs that aren't real, talking about money, stocks, high-brow stuff a country cracker from Georgia certainly couldn't relate to.

"We know you're the brains behind this operation, and next year when Sampson's lease is over, we'll probably take over. We do have some ideas about what we'll do with the place, and it will be much better for us and the downtown revitalization efforts."

"Interesting."

Flattery will certainly *not* get Bennett or his family anywhere with me. I just wished he would snip or clip his ear hairs. Most men got them at some point, and some did something about them and some didn't. Bennett obviously hadn't done a thing with his, though he only had a few that were long and one curled over the lobe. I imagined it would tickle and he probably should've noticed it. Maybe he didn't care.

I didn't know what else to say. I certainly didn't like what I was hearing, but I did admire his ability to show his true colors on the front end, which, quite frankly, showed me he was not the shrewd businessman he, or Sampson, thought he was and probably not much like his family. A true shrewd businessman wouldn't have given up the end goal on the front end of a conversation. I likened his behavior to a football player and the line of scrimmage saying, "Hey, you on the other team, I've got a bad knee," or "We are gonna win this game by throwing the ball because our wide receivers all have hangovers." Bennett was showing his cards up front, and he didn't know how loyal I had been to Sampson.

"You can probably get in on some of the action, if you want." He smirked.

"I'll certainly think about it." What I intended to think about was meeting with Sampson, giving him the play-by-play, so he could form his best defense. I had already started thinking about defense.

"Your wife is a teacher, right?"

"Yes." They'd done their homework, like good politicians.

"Does she want to get into administration? We could probably suggest she be given a much higher paying job."

"I don't think she does. She really enjoys teaching."

I was disgusted that with all the budget issues that are constantly blasted on local news channels about the school system, teachers not being able to buy supplies, fundraisers dipping into the pockets of parents who already pay enough taxes to purchase needed equipment, that Bennett and those like him were part of the reason there were budget problems, using positions and high salaries as pawns for their financial and political games.

"It is an honorable profession."

"Yes, it is." I wondered what Bennett would know about honor.

"The second question I had is if you think we could get a block of rooms for a fraternity reunion we're having over at Vandy."

I wanted to knock him out. Already, he was cutting into the profit by wanting discounts for friends. "We can probably work out some sort of discount."

"I wanted to get them free. I can give you the fraternity foundation information, so the business could get a tax break from charity."

"I may need to talk to Sampson about that."

"I prefer you work this out without mentioning it to him. I certainly wouldn't want you to do anything that might jeopardize your position."

I'd bet my last dollar on him not wanting me to jeopardize my position with his family. People like Bennett and his family would be the first to see me walk out the door when they took over. I would be too much of a threat for them. Of course, they wouldn't do it immediately. They'd lay in wait, being nice and inviting me to socials. Then, after they had a true understanding of the operation, they would want to change things, cut services and increase profits. That's when the disagreements would begin. Then they would give me my walking papers.

I simply said, "I'll see what I can do."

"The other thing I need to know is if the organization supports any charities locally."

"Yes, Mr. Sampson has always supported local charities. He annually gives money to the homeless shelter, the victims of domestic violence, the animal shelter, American Cancer Society, and the children's hospital at Vanderbilt. There may be others, but those are the ones I can think of at the moment. In fact, he and Earline have received awards and have been recognized for their charitable contributions."

"As a whole, does the organization support charities through, say, payroll deduction?"

"No, not that I know of." As two housekeepers pushed a cart by, he paused, nodded at them, and I told them, "Good morning."

Once they had passed, Bennett moved closer toward me. "I would like for you to help me by getting the organization to support my fraternity, through one of its subsidiary charity names, by asking staff to donate by payroll deduction. I feel certain this can be accomplished with your support. Everyone likes you."

I no longer wanted to hit Bennett. I wanted to shove him into a room, lift him onto a shower hook, where the plush robes were hung, and bludgeon him with the largest object I could find, locking him in the room to slowly bleed and fade from existence. "The majority of the staff aren't paid that well, and I'm sure what little money they earn goes to support their own charities, primarily their churches."

"Once I bring you the materials we've had a local marketing firm design, then I'm sure you'll see that they come around."

At this point, I simply nodded. I was too disgusted to respond to Bennett, and like my mama had taught me, if you can't say something nice, don't say nothing at all. "I need to get back to my office," I said.

"Okay, we'll talk later." He extended his hand, and I took it, gripped it too tight, and smiled. Bennett seemed a little sullen, like a dog that's been scolded with his tail curled between his legs.

I walked back to my office and noticed the message light flashing on my phone. Checking messages, I felt an adrenaline rush from a message from the Apalachee, asking that I return the call. Another was from Jaden saying she was just checking in and I didn't need to return the call. First, I returned the call to the human resources department at the Apalachee, and the young lady said they would be interested in my coming for an interview as early as Friday of this week, and I told her yes, and she also asked if the owner could go ahead and check my references and I told her yes. I asked who the current owner was and she said Lola Bertinelli-Smith was the owner, that her father had once owned the hotel, but he had passed away a few years back and Ms. Lola had taken over the operation. This seemed to ring true with Sampson's story, and I was excited that old friends would talk once more, but I did not tell the human resources lady that. I thanked her for her phone call, told her I was honored to be a candidate.

I then called Jaden and asked her if she could take off the next two days to go with me to Tallahassee. She said she probably could. She'd just have to give a substitute a call and get lessons organized. I was kind of surprised at her reaction. Her wanting to do that, I mean, for it was a rarity she would take off work even if she didn't feel well. I figured she wanted to talk to her mama, maybe even look for a job herself, though that thinking was probably putting the cart before the horse.

I found Sampson in the café and told him the Apalachee had called, and if Lola Bertinelli-Smith was his former girl-friend, then she'd be the one calling. He smiled and nodded. I told him I need to take off Thursday and Friday to go back down there, and he said that was fine. I knew Sampson would put in a good word for me, but I also knew part of him was worried about me leaving, what the employees would think, what would happen with Bennett. I did mention to him that I had met and talked with Bennett and had some inkling of what their family intentions were. I'd like to help him with some strategies.

When I got home, Jaden was already home and packing for us. I was fascinated by her new-found energy and the glow that seemed to surround her. She found a substitute to replace her and there were no problems with her principal. Jaden said her doctor's appointment wasn't until next week, so she felt okay about leaving.

"If this works out, Max, then we need to get it done. I'm not moving if I'm big as a house."

"I imagine if I do get the job, they would want me within a month. That's not a lot of time. Would you want to rent the condo or sell it?"

"I would rather sell it. We'd need the equity for a good down payment on a home in Tallahassee, but if we couldn't sell it, then I would rent it, but only through a realtor. I wouldn't want to come back and forth to deal with it."

"Sure," I agreed.

We both ate some prepackaged frozen dinners, which weren't low in calories or sodium. They were simply low in portions, which is how many famous people said they'd lost weight, though neither of us needed to lose any weight. In fact, I'd probably get up in the night to get a snack, it was so unfulfilling. After dinner, with the Accord packed and ready to go early the next morning, I checked the time to see if Mama and Daddy would be home from church. They were on Eastern Time and we were on Central, and since it was nine in the evening, I knew they should be back from church. Mama answered on the third ring.

"Did I wake you up?"

"Lord, no, I was watching a movie on Lifetime. Your daddy is in his room watching the History channel."

"How was the meeting at church tonight?"

"I think it went all right. We booted him out, but some of the congregation walked out with him. They might start a new church, and that's fine. They'll be back sooner or later when the truth comes out."

"Did it get ugly?"

"Not too bad. Your daddy read part of the constitution and called for a vote. One woman who lives out in the country, her daddy is a tobacco farmer, stood up and said something about dirty laundry, but no one really knew what she was talking about since no one has seen her in a month of Sundays. Majority raised their hands to let him go, and he walked out the door with Mrs. Mason trailing behind. Then a group of them walked out, too, including Mrs. Yates, and even your cousin Doug. I think your daddy was disappointed he went with them."

"I'm disappointed, too."

"Well, if Doug's got any sense at all, and Lord knows he's killed off some of his brain cells, bless his heart, he won't put his faith in a man."

"That's true. Well, so ya'll are okay?"

"Sure."

"Well, Jaden and I are coming down there tomorrow. You think it'd be all right if we stay out at Aunt Ophelia's house?"

"Of course, it would. Something wrong? Why're ya'll coming?"

"I've got a job interview at the Apalachee Hotel in Tallahassee."

"Praise the Lord. I can't wait to tell your daddy."

"Mama, it's just an interview. Don't mean I'll get the job."

"Well, if you do, will ya'll live here and commute, or you think you might live in Tallahassee?"

"I imagine we'd live in Tallahassee."

"Good. I could come shop all day then spend the night."

"Well, don't plan any trips just yet."

"Okay, ya'll be careful."

"Thanks. See you tomorrow."

"Why don't you be over here in time for supper? I'll fix something good."

"That's fine with me. See you then."

I told Jaden Mama wanted us to eat with them tomorrow night when we got there, and she said that was fine. "I'm sure I'll gain some weight while we're down there," she said.

Since it was after nine o'clock, Jaden called her parents on her cell phone, because it was free, and they, too, were excited we were coming home. She agreed we'd eat with them on Friday night.

The next morning, we got up early to beat the rush hour traffic in Nashville. Though traffic in a major city is always heavy, we were going against the influx of commuters, so it wasn't too bad. We stopped at Monteagle to use the restroom and made it to Atlanta after rush hour there. I asked Jaden if she wanted to stop at Chick-Fil-A, but she didn't. She wanted to stop at The Varsity downtown near Georgia Tech for lunch. I almost ran off the road.

"Jaden, you want to eat at The Varsity?"

"Max, I'm craving a chili cheese dog, a fried apple pie, and a Coke."

I laughed. "Oh, I'm all for going to The Varsity. We

should've become pregnant many years ago and several times, too, if that would have made you go The Varsity."

"Well, I'm sure all this will pass."

"I hope not."

"One of us has got to raise this child. It's harder if your arteries are clogged."

"Look at that damned eighteen wheeler. He just cut that car off. It's a miracle they didn't slam into someone. Oh, I hate driving in Atlanta."

"Yeah, I don't think I'd want to live here, but it is a beautiful city. You know which exit to take?"

"I think I can remember how to get there. I think it's the same one as Georgia Tech."

We pulled off, ordered our cravings, and we were stuffed. I wanted to eat another, or get one to take with me, but I didn't. It was difficult driving to Pavo after eating such a lunch because we were both tired. Jaden propped her feet on the dashboard, reclined in her seat, and fell asleep.

She wanted to listen to Enya, and that music didn't help my tiredness either, but I let it play and thought about my interview. I didn't worry too much about it. I certainly had the experience and could probably answer any questions they asked.

When we got to my parent's house, Jaden woke up. "I can't believe we're already here."

"You sure you don't want to tell our parents you're pregnant?"

"No, I think we should wait a while."

We got out, walked under the carport, and into the house. Mama was in the kitchen stirring field peas cooked in chicken broth with bacon, and Daddy was in the recliner reading the newspaper.

"Hey," Mama said.

Daddy put his paper down and got up. "Can't believe ya'll are here already. You must've made good time."

"We did," I said.

"Jaden, you look great," Mama told her. "Like you're glowing or something."

"I'm just excited about Max's interview."

"So are we," Daddy stated satisfactorily. "I thought I'd call a few people in Tallahassee if you want me to."

"No, that's okay. Mr. Sampson knows the owners. I'm sure he'll give me a good reference."

We ate peas, fried chicken, biscuits, corn-on-the-cob, and for dessert, Mama baked a chocolate cake, fifteen layers. It was delicious, and we all went to the den and plopped on the furniture for a while. The news was on, and once again, the Gulf of Mexico had a tropical storm brewing that might turn into a hurricane by the middle of the week.

"They've had enough hurricanes in Florida."

"Sure have," Daddy said. "I talked with a fellow a week or so ago at the post office who has a brother who lives in Pensacola, and they are paying so much for insurance, they're thinking of selling and moving here."

"Well, I'd hate for another hurricane to hit the Gulf," Mama said. "They've all suffered so much these last few years. We do need some rain, though."

Jaden and I said we probably ought to get to Aunt Ophelia's house, unpack, and get a good night's sleep before my interview.

"You'll do fine," Daddy responded.

"Sure will," agreed Mama. "You always do."

"I'll let ya'll know how it goes."

"You want to come eat tomorrow?"

"No, we're gonna eat with Jaden's parents tomorrow night."

"When ya'll gonna leave?"

"I think we'll head on back Saturday morning some time."

"I would invite ya'll to stay and go to church, but I don't know if we'll have service Sunday or not," Mama said.

"We will have a service," Daddy reassured. "We called a retired preacher from over around Valdosta who's gonna come serve as interim until we find someone."

"Oh, good," Mama sighed in relief.

"Thanks again for a delicious supper," Jaden stated.

"Honey, you're welcome. Anytime."

Jaden and I hugged Mama and Daddy and got in the Accord to make the short drive to Aunt Ophelia's house. The house inside looked clean, but the yard did need mowing, and I thought I might do that before I left. We turned on the attic fan, and I lugged our overnight bag and garment bag up to the spare bedroom. Once settled, Jaden and I sat in the porch swing and rocked for a while until the sun began to go down. I told her about Buddy wanting to buy the place and the snake, and she moved closer to me.

"Max, if the baby's a girl, I think I want to name her Ophelia."

"Really?"

"Yes. I want to honor your aunt, and I think your family would really like that. Mine, too, for that matter. Everyone loved her, and she was a strong woman. I think the origin of the name is to help."

"That certainly did fit her."

"Yes, it did."

Chapter
12

When I awoke, I could smell breakfast in the kitchen. Jaden had awakened before me for once and was cooking. I told her she didn't have to get up and cook, and she said she wanted to. She said she was craving some "real" breakfast. I wondered if any of Aunt Ophelia's food would still be good, but Jaden assured me it was all fresh. I figured Mama had come by and stocked up a bit. She also said she forgot about the peacocks, how loud their screams were, how beautiful they looked. Having been away for so long, I admit that I enjoyed the screams, but growing up, I'd always likened their screams to what I seemed to hear from old maid school teachers and church ladies who screamed rules and hushes at "mean old boys," but meant no harm at all. I had come to see their behavior in adulthood as flirty passive-aggressive.

We ate breakfast and I told Jaden I should get ready for the interview, so I took a shower and dressed. When I came back downstairs, Jaden was in the porch swing, sipping coffee.

"You want to go to Tallahassee with me or stay here?"

"I think I'll go, drop you off for the interview, and do some shopping."

"I guess I could call you on your cell when I'm done."

"That'll work."

"We could get a bite to eat. Let's go to Good Time Charlie's."

"That does sound good."

We'd not been to the Cajun restaurant Good Time Charlie's in a few years, but we loved their gumbo, their blues music, and I loved the horse trough toilet in the restroom filled with ice on which men urinated. The furnishings—booths, chairs, tile, curtains—were all red, and though I didn't drink a lot of beer anymore, their collection was extensive.

"Have a cup of coffee, and I'll be ready shortly."

Jaden went inside to take a shower and dress while I sipped more coffee in the swing. When she returned, she had on sandals, a yellow sundress, and a purse to match. Jaden was always beautiful, but she seemed even more beautiful now that she was pregnant.

"You ready?"

"Sure, let's go."

"You nervous?"

"No, for some reason, I'm not."

"You shouldn't be. I may run by the Board of Education office, too, while you're interviewing. See if they have anything."

"That's a good idea, but do you want to work with the baby?"

"Part of me doesn't and part of me does. Too bad they don't have part-time teachers. Probably be less burnout if they did. Maybe they'll have something part-time."

I got up, set my coffee cup in the sink, and grabbed my briefcase. Jaden grabbed her purse, and we got in the Accord for the hour or so drive to Tallahassee via Highway 319. The drive to Tallahassee was beautiful with historical plantations dotting the landscape with long leaf pines and Live Oak trees with Spanish moss. The plantations today were primarily hunting plantations, and even though I hadn't been hunting on any of them, I had friends who worked them or had been there to hunt. Traffic picked up once we neared Tallahassee, and we drove straight to downtown, where Jaden dropped me off in front of the Apalachee. I was five minutes early.

The Apalachee was clean and well-maintained, and the

doorman welcomed me and held the door. The clerk directed me to the human resources office, and I walked down the ceramic tiled hallway, my Johnson and Murphy shoes clopping against the tile.

"Good morning, I'm Max Peacock," I announced, and the human resources manager stood and firmly shook my hand.

"Come on back to the conference room. Ms. Bertinelli-Smith will be here shortly. Can I get you some coffee or water?"

"I'll take some water, if you don't mind."

Historical photos lined the walls, and I glanced at each one. In one black and white shot, a small girl held her daddy's hand while her daddy shook hands with President Roosevelt. I imagined it was Ms. Bertinelli-Smith and they looked proud and happy, and the hotel then, with different landscaping, seemed timeless. The door creaked opened, and a woman dressed in a dark suit greeted me. She was beautiful with tanned skin and dark hair and eyes. I supposed she was about sixty, given Sampson's age, but she looked in her mid-forties.

"Max Peacock, I presume. It's a pleasure to meet you. I'm Lola Bertinelli-Smith."

"It's a pleasure to meet you, too."

"Please, have a seat."

I did and we talked about business, my experience in management for over an hour. She was attentive and kept focused on me the entire time, slightly smiling from time to time. When we finished, Ms. Bertinelli-Smith, said, "I talked with Mr. Sampson, Max, and he is very complimentary of you and the work you've done in Nashville."

"Thanks, if I do get this position, I will miss him more than I can say. He's taught me a lot."

"Did you know we used to date?"

"He mentioned he knew you, but didn't go into detail."

"I think it's ironic he ended up in the hotel business, too, but he did tell me of the difficulty he's having."

"Yes, it's pretty bad, apparently. I can't imagine the stress he's under."

"Well, I'd like to offer you the position."

"You're kidding? Just like that? No follow-up interview or we'll call you after we finish interviewing?"

"We had a few local candidates, and we had an internal candidate, who has done an excellent job as food and beverage manager, but she doesn't have the experience you do. I didn't advertise nationally due to expense, but I really do need someone who knows the business. If you take the position, you'll have to work with the food and beverage manager. I doubt she'll be a problem for you at all, but still, I'm sure she'll be disappointed."

"Of course. That wouldn't be a problem. I am honored, and I'll accept."

"You don't even know how much I'm offering, but I'll definitely match your salary and offer you ten thousand more than what Sampson is paying. Of course, I can't pay you the bonuses he has, but I can offer you something else."

"What's that?"

"The hotel itself."

"What do you mean?"

"If you like working at the Apalachee, I'll begin giving you stock as bonuses. My husband and I have no children. My husband has cancer and may be here another year, if we're lucky. I won't be able to keep up the pace and can't right now and help care for him. Anyway, I'll retire at some point, and I'll retain stock, but I would only want to retain stock if I knew my stock would be worth something. I'll make you a good deal on the place, if you want to buy it at some point, and the land is owned, not leased." She smiled and added, "I just don't want to turn this over to a corporation, who would let it go down and raise the prices. We've had a good reputation for a very long time. Sooner or later, people will move away from the corporations."

"I appreciate it. If there's anything I can do to help with your husband, please let me know. My wife, Jaden, will be off for the summer, since she's a teacher, and she might be willing to help you out some." I wondered if I should have volunteered Jaden for something, especially with her being pregnant. She certainly didn't have a problem volunteering me, but the minute it left my mouth, I felt bad. Most people, though, don't mean it, and certainly most people don't take others up on such offers.

"Thank you. So, when do you want to start?"

"I'd like to stay at least two weeks to help Mr. Sampson get adjusted and get everything in order. Then I could be here."

"Are you going to commute from Pavo or live in Tallahassee?"

"I think we'll live in Tallahassee, but I may have to commute until we can close in Tennessee and close here in Tallahassee. Jaden and I both love it here."

"My sister is a realtor. She'll find you a nice home and something worth the money, if you want her to. Here's her card."

"That's great. I'd like to call her, but we may search online first and come back next weekend to see places after we've narrowed the search," I said.

"Okay, then, why don't you let me take you on a tour?"

"That sounds great."

Ms. Bertinelli-Smith asked if I would call her Lola and I said I would. She took me on a tour of the property, inside and out, but it was so much more than just a tour; it was a walk through time. I made a mental note to put together a history of the property in book form as soon as I came on board. She was such a kind woman, and she reminded me of Aunt Ophelia in some ways—mainly her soft spoken tone combined with her shrewdness and pragmatism. After the tour was over, she took me back to the Human Resources office where she told them to give me the paperwork to complete regarding taxes and benefits. She told me to have a safe trip back to Tennessee and that she would see me in a couple of weeks. She needed to get home to see about her husband. I took the paperwork to a computer room for guests near the lobby and called Jaden on the cell.

"How'd it go?"

"I got it."

"Already? That was quick. I'll be back in a few minutes then. I'm not too far from there now."

The old black man who held the door for me on the way out looked familiar. He smiled and told me to have a good day, and I echoed his sentiment. Jaden kissed me, told me how excited she was. She couldn't believe I had been hired on the spot. We talked for a while about Lola, the hotel, and her offer about owning it one day.

Jaden said, "This was all just meant to be."

We drove down Pensacola street, went to Good Time Charlie's, and had a shrimp po boy sandwich and a cup of gumbo. We decided to drive around Tallahassee a bit to get a sense of neighborhoods, we went to the mall to look at baby items, and we drove by the Chamber of Commerce to pick up a newcomer's packet. Well into the afternoon, we decided to go on back to Jaden's parents, and she called them on her cell phone. She told them about my getting the job, and I could hear her mother's delight as she held the cell away from her face.

Once at Ed and Doris' house, they came out to meet us at the car. We parked in the circular drive, and Doris raised her eyebrows. "Jaden, what's different?"

"Nothing, Mama," she said.

"Yes, there is. You're pregnant, aren't you?"

"I have an appointment next week to confirm and get checked. How did you know?"

"Women know these things. It's like a glow. Congratulations, honey."

"Thanks."

Ed and Doris both embraced Jaden, then turned to me. Ed shook my hand and Doris hugged me, dabbing at the corners of her eyes.

"It's about time, you two," Ed said.

"Are ya'll going to tell anyone? If you are, then I need to tell my parents. I'd never hear the end of it if someone else knew before they did."

"Jaden? What do you want us to do?"

"I'd prefer we wait just to make sure everything is all right."

"Okay, then, we won't say a word," said Doris. "Come on in. I've got a salad and your daddy grilled Delmonico steaks. I've got some baked potatoes and I made blueberry crunch for dessert."

"My favorite," Jaden said. "Well, at least the baby is eating well."

"So are we," I said.

"Max, I guess congratulations are in order. Tell us about this job."

We sat for dinner, and as we ate, I told them about the issues at Sampson's hotel in Nashville, and I told them about Ms. Bertinelli-Smith, her offer, and the old connection between the two.

"It's a small world," said Doris.

"Yes, it is," I replied.

"How did you hear about the job?" Ed asked.

"Interestingly, Effie, an old woman who cooks at the Thomasville Grill, where I used to work when it was called Tasty World years ago, told me her cousin works at the Apalachee, and she told me about it. I didn't even think to look up her cousin when I was there. I guess I will now."

"Effie used to work for us part-time," said Doris. "She stopped when Jaden was about four and went to work full time on the evening shift at the restaurant. She had a newborn herself at that time and wanted to stay home with her during the day while her husband worked. I think he worked at the coat factory in Thomasville. Is that right, Ed?"

"I think so."

"Jaden used to love her. At one point, I think Jaden connected more with Effie than she did with me."

"I didn't know that," I said. "It really is a small world. Jaden, you never told me Effie was your nanny."

"Max, I can barely remember those years, but I do remember her and how much I liked her. For the longest time, when I smelled someone smoking, I associated it with pleasant memories because she smoked."

"Never in the house, though," said Doris. "Only when she took you outside to your little blow-up pool or the swing set."

"So have ya'll thought of names?" Ed asked.

"If it's a girl, we'll name her Ophelia. I don't know what we'll name it if it's a boy," Jaden said.

"How about Max, Junior," I asked.

"No," Jaden said. "And I've already told you no once. No juniors or seconds."

"Max, did you know this when you were here last week? If you did, you're a pretty good actor," Doris said.

"No, in fact, Jaden hadn't been feeling well and went to the doctor, thinking it was sinus drainage making her sick to her stomach. It turned out that wasn't the case. You can imagine my surprise when the doctor called and told me to tell her not to take the sinus medication they'd given her."

"Also goes to show you that half the time they don't know what the hell they're doing," Ed said. "They just write prescriptions depending on which pharmaceutical sales rep gives them the most samples or the best kick-backs."

"Aunt Ophelia would've said the same thing," I said.

"Your aunt was a smart woman," Ed affirmed. "I'm glad she was able to hold onto that farm. Helping all those people over the years paid off for her."

"How's that?" I asked.

"Some of them paid her. She didn't do it for the money, but if someone offers you a gift, you ought to take it."

"I didn't know she got paid."

"I don't think it was a lot, Max, but it was enough to pay the taxes all those years. Of course, her parents left her some money. In fact, as I recall, they had some oil stock that became quite lucrative over the years. She might've sold some of that, too, to make ends meet."

"The more I'm here, the more I learn," I said. "Just goes to show that you never know everything you think you do."

Once finished with dessert, Jaden and I decided to go on back to Aunt Ophelia's and get a good night's sleep before we traveled back on Saturday. We just wanted to rest on Sunday and get everything prepared for the week. We said our goodbyes and hugged Ed and Doris, and as we drove to Aunt Ophelia's twilight had set in, and fireflies flickered in the fields. Fireflies were an oddity to us now, having lived so long in the big city that we didn't experience their iridescent glow. It was a peaceful feeling to know that we were coming home, or at least close to home, and I imagined Tallahassee would have fireflies, too, since it was still a small capitol town when compared to Nashville, while other cities in Florida outranked Tallahassee in population such as Miami, Jacksonville, Tampa, and Orlando.

When we got to Aunt Ophelia's, Jaden said she wasn't feeling well, that her stomach was doing somersaults. She went upstairs and laid down on the bed, and while part of me wanted to snoop through the trunk to read more letters, I decided that would have to wait. First, I needed to call Mama and Daddy and let them know about the job.

Daddy answered, "Hello?"

"Hey. What're ya'll doing?"

"Your mama has gone to bed. Her stomach is upset from eating some more fried green tomatoes. I told her not to eat them."

"She's not having any other problems, is she?"

"Not now."

"What was wrong?"

"I don't know, really. Just don't feel good much anymore, and I heard the more blood you get to your head the better you feel, so I jacked the foot of our bed up with some bricks. That way, blood will rush to our heads while we sleep, and I figured that would make her feel better."

"I've never heard that before. Did it work?"

"Oh yeah, it worked. I never told her I jacked up the bed, and she's feeling better and don't even know it. I feel a lot better myself. Of course, I always feel good. I plan to live to be one hundred, at least."

"I hope so. Listen, I just wanted ya'll to know that I got the job in Tallahassee at the Apalachee. Jaden and I are excited about it."

"That's great. I had a feeling you might. It's a good place."

"Have you been there?"

"No, but my grandparents stayed there quite a bit when

they visited family in Tallahassee. Sometimes, they stayed for a while, from what I remember about Ophelia telling me."

"Really? That's amazing. I wonder if they knew the Bertinelli family."

"I don't know. Who owns it now?"

"Lola Bertinelli-Smith. She's probably in her sixties, but her daddy owned it and ran it for a long time, maybe forty or fifty years. I don't know."

"He probably knew Ophelia. Maybe knew Papa and Grandma, too."

"I'll have to remember to ask."

"You want me to wake your mama?"

"No, Daddy, let her rest and get some blood in her head. Tell her tomorrow. That'll start her day off on the right foot. We're gonna leave early and head back, but I'll need to start in a couple of weeks or so, and I'll keep you updated."

"Ya'll gonna sell your condo or rent it?"

"I don't know. We'll see what we can get for it first. We need to hire movers."

"I don't mind coming and helping ya'll move."

"No, I think we'll just hire it done. It's a tax write-off." While I appreciated his offer, I knew Daddy didn't want to drive to Nashville and fight the traffic.

"You're welcome to move into Ophelia's."

"I think we'll buy a place in Tallahassee."

"Tallahassee's expensive. It'll be cheaper for ya'll to live at Ophelia's for free."

"That's true, but I think Jaden would prefer to live there for now. We might get a condo or something and then come stay at Ophelia's on the weekend. Of course, we may have to stay at Aunt Ophelia's until we find a place."

"That's a thought. Well, ya'll be careful and call us when you get home, so your mama won't worry."

"We will. Talk to you tomorrow."

Daddy and I hung up the phone, and I pulled out my laptop and logged onto the exchange server to check my work email. There were some junk emails from Thursday and Friday morning, which I deleted, but there was an afternoon email from Sampson titled "new job." The email read:

> Max, my boy. Congratulations on the new job. Lola called me and told me she was going to steal you away, and reluctantly, I told her you'd be better off. I know she needs you soon, so if you'll just work a week or two longer here, clear up any loose ends, then I'll let you go. While I do hate to see you go, Earline, too, part of me is excited about seeing Bennett Fillmore work his ass off. I plan to put him to work until he can't take it anymore, and maybe, just maybe, if I can run him off, then they'll back off from taking over the property. It might just work. I might be getting old, but I'm still smart and love a good fight. Ya'll be careful coming back. S.

It was a relief to know that Sampson already knew about my getting the job, and it was a pleasure to read that he had mustered up something inside himself that would fight to the last with the Fillmore family. I truly hoped he won, and actually, I began to think of ways I might assist in those efforts in my last couple of weeks.

Jaden slept soundly, and when we got up, I told her about Sampson's email. She was relieved to hear that he already knew. We showered, dressed in t-shirts, shorts and tennis shoes, and got on the road before sun up. Jaden slept most of the trip, still not feeling too well, and we stopped in Calhoun and got a grilled turkey sandwich at Cracker Barrel. When we got back to Nashville, I unloaded the car and started a load of laundry.

Jaden was still feeling sick, and she wanted homemade chicken soup from Demo's Steak and Spaghetti House downtown. I called, placed a to-go order, and went to pick it up. While we were eating, Jaden got up from the table and ran to the half-bath just off the great room and began gagging, hugging the toilet. I asked if she needed my help and she said no, so I continued to eat. When she washed her face, she walked back in and told me she was going to lie down. I asked if she wasn't going to eat her soup, I would, and she said that was fine. I didn't realize it until I had said it that it probably sounded a bit cold.

After watching television for a while, and the news, I went to bed, and Jaden was snoring, something she didn't used to do. I fell asleep and was stunned when the alarm went off at five o'clock in the morning because it seemed like I had just laid down.

I left before Jaden, and she was feeling somewhat better. When I got to work, I was surprised Sampson had already told some of the staff, and word had spread quickly. In fact, Bennett Fillmore had heard, and he came to my office rather nervously and congratulated me on my position.

"I guess you'll assume most of my duties, Bennett, since Sampson can't really afford to hire a replacement after hiring you."

"I guess," he smirked.

"Well, if you need anything, I'm just a phone call away. Oh, and I didn't get a chance to check into that block of rooms for you, or the charity business. You might want to talk to Sampson."

"Maybe," he said.

Bennett slunk away, and I felt good that he seemed somewhat defeated even though that probably wasn't the way I should have felt. I hadn't seen Sampson yet, but that was typical, since he came and went at will.

I called a realtor I knew from Rotary to meet with Jaden and me about selling the condo, and I also called a couple of movers to come over the next morning to give me estimates on the costs involved. Finally, I called Jaden to let her know what I was doing, so she wouldn't worry, and she was appreciative, having had a rough day with her nausea. I checked schedules, did a walk-about, placed some orders, and returned some phone calls to tour companies that felt they were too important to deal with reservationists and would only deal with the manager. I left a little early to get home and straighten the condo before the realtor came so Jaden wouldn't have to worry with it. I don't know why, really, except that when people come to your house, you don't want it looking too rough. I guess I learned that from Mama and I did think it made some sort of difference. It seemed you get more compliments that way. Of course, realtors in general are going to be complimentary because they want the business, so I guess it didn't matter.

Chapter
13

Jaden and I met with the realtor and signed a contract. Surprisingly, we listed the condo for fifty thousand more than we paid for it because prices had risen in Nashville, and the realtor believed we would get it. She also reassured us that she worked for us, that if there was something we felt needed to be done, she was just a phone call away. Personally, I thought all realtors worked only for themselves. Fortunately for us, time was on our side as it was currently a "seller's market" in Nashville, which made us both feel good. Realtor Sandra Pate agreed to have the condo inspected at her expense, thinking that would make for an easier sell, and we told her we appreciated it. Of course, it only costs two hundred dollars, but typically, the buyer paid that expense before purchase. Apparently, Sandra was in cahoots with a friend's husband who had gone into the home inspection business.

The next morning, Jaden went on to work, and I stayed behind to meet with movers. I was astounded at the costs associated with packing and moving—extra charges for boxes, tape, packing, and so on. It was the add-on costs that always stick it to you; the majority of the costs, however, were because of the rising gas prices that politicians had been either unable to control or, as I suspected, purposefully *didn't* control since their investments were in oil. Nonetheless, I felt we simply didn't have time to deal with the moving, and I certainly didn't want Jaden doing anything that might jeopardize the baby's health. Of course, I couldn't handle it by myself, and I didn't want her parents or my parents coming to assist.

That evening, Jaden and I searched online, looking at condos and homes in Tallahassee. Not only could we narrow a search by neighborhood, price, number of bedrooms, and so on, but we could get average utility costs, taxes, and most importantly, make sure no sexual predators lived in the neighborhoods. What I think we came to love most about looking at places online was the ability to actually enter the house and see rooms through virtual tours. We found ourselves turning off computer speakers, so we didn't have to listen to the music or the realtors, and although most of the homes looked clean, we found some who clearly were trying to cover up a carpet spot, a missing kitchen cabinet knob, a burn mark on the countertop by strategically placing small things in areas where one wouldn't normally place them—a stool not near a chair or a trivet not near the stove top. We found several that were in our range, and we printed off the Multiple Listing sheets for those we wanted to see. We planned to just move into Aunt Ophelia's house, store the furniture, and meet with Lola's sister to narrow our list. We also believed we could take our time and get the best buy for our money since we had a place to stay. We were lucky in that sense, too, for most people had to make quick decisions and move, not giving them time to shop more wisely.

Jaden went to the doctor that week and discovered she was two months pregnant and was advised not to travel much. She explained to the doctor that we were in the process of moving to Tallahassee, so he recommended a friend in that area who was a reputable doctor. In the meantime, she had an ultrasound, and based on what they saw, they predicted a little girl, though they wouldn't commit to the prediction. Part of us wanted to schedule an amnio once we met the doctor in Tallahassee to make sure there weren't any genetic issues, but of course, we couldn't get them to check for a particular mental illness, since we didn't know what Great Aunt Helen had.

That night, I called Mama and Daddy and told them

our plans. They were both on the phone.

"That's fine," Daddy said. "You can stay long as you want."

"It won't be more than a month or so. I have some more news," I told them.

"What?" Mama asked.

"Jaden and I are going to have a baby girl."

Mama yelled and Daddy said, "Congratulations."

"I already knew it," Mama sniffed.

"How'd you know?" I asked.

"I could tell when Jaden walked in. She had gained a little weight, but she had the glow. I'd be the last person on earth to tell her she had gained some weight."

I decided not to tell Jaden about the weight gain remark. "Funny, her mama said the same thing about the glow."

"When did ya'll tell her?"

"I'm not sure when Jaden talked to her," I lied. I made a mental note to tell Jaden to call her Mama and tell her not to say anything in case Mama saw her in town and they talked. I didn't want her mad.

"So have you got a name yet?"

"We're naming her Ophelia."

"That's great," Daddy said.

"That's a good name, and your aunt would be proud," Mama said. "I'll get a church shower planned for when ya'll get down here."

"Don't go to any trouble," I said.

"It ain't no trouble."

"Well, I better go. We need to get busy around here, but we'll see you this weekend."

"Sounds good," Daddy said.

"Did Mama already hang up?"

"Yes, she did."

"Something wrong?"

"No, I think she's crying. She grabbed some Kleenex and went to the bathroom."

"Why's she crying?"

"I don't know. I guess because she's happy. Cries all the time, if you ask me. Maybe I need to jack the bed up some more."

"Is she going through the change?"

"Going through something," Daddy muttered.

"How's the church doing?"

"Good. The interim preacher's a hit, and we hear Reverend Mason confessed to his wife. Some saw her loading suitcases in the car and driving out of town. I heard Mrs. Yates put her house up for sale and is moving back to Atlanta. She might have a hard time selling it."

"What will Mason do now? He's lost both his wife and his girlfriend, his job, and a house, since it's owned by the church."

"I don't know what he'll do, but that's his problem. I guess he got himself into the mess and he'll have to get himself out. That's life. He's got to be out of the house in a couple of weeks, so he better get a move on."

"Think he'll go back to preaching somewhere?"

"Not in a Baptist church. Maybe he'll become a Methodist preacher."

"How's Doug?"

"Well, I think Doug is doing all right. He actually came back to church this week and sat with us. I guess his following Mason didn't last too long."

"That's good."

"I appreciate everything, Daddy," I said.

"You're welcome. Look forward to having ya'll around. Maybe we can do some fishing some time soon at the pond."

"I'd like that."

"See you next week. Ya'll be careful."

"Okay."

We hung up the phone, and I told Jaden about Mama. I was worried about her, but Jaden said Mama probably needed to go to her doctor and see about taking hormones, that her mama had taken them and got a lot better after starting a regimen. I also told Jaden she needed to call her mama and tell her not to tell my mama when we'd told them the news about the baby. I didn't want Mama mad or upset with us. She agreed and called her mama on the cell and told her that, and then told her to call my mama and suggest hormones, not directly, but indirectly after pleasant conversation about health as most Southerners tend to do.

The next week, we had some boxes in our garage and tried to keep the condo constantly picked up and clean, which is a chore, so possible buyers could see it as pristine as possible. Before the week was over, we had a low ball offer on the condo, and we countered and offered some money back at closing. The realtors duked it out, or so Ms. Pate said. I no more believe they duked it out than a man in the moon. They simply figured up how much each of them would make. Within a day or so, we had a solid contract.

Jaden and I were very pleased, however, there was an inspection, which revealed some minor items that needed repair. I didn't want to repair a thing. When one buys a "used" residence, buyers shouldn't expect everything to be perfect, but I had the hotel maintenance man come over and do the minor repairs, and he gave me a fair price. I was fortunate to have been able to get him to do it since any maintenance work was expensive and the people who did that sort of work were difficult to locate and not always reliable.

My last week at work, Sampson had a buffet reception for me in the restaurant and had invited Jaden. She didn't eat much, but everyone else did. Earline came, as did a number of folks from the Rotary Club downtown. Anytime there was free food, you could count on a crowd of people. Sampson made a brief speech, gave me a gold watch that I wasn't sure I would wear, and he was ecstatic. I knew he was happy for me, but for some reason, I thought there was something more to it. As the reception wound down, he walked over and said, "I'll miss you, boy."

"Same here. I appreciate everything."

"And I'll be coming to visit you in Tallahassee, too."

"Have you and Earline already planned a trip?"

"Nah, but I'll come visit in a few months. I'd like to see Lola again."

"I'm sure Lola would enjoy seeing you and Earline, too," I said.

"Not Earline, just me. What Earline don't know won't

hurt her." Sampson winked, and while I knew he was kidding at some level, I felt he probably wasn't at another level. Just because boys physically grow into teens into men, into old men doesn't mean their minds do and the image of a rendez-vous between Sampson and my new boss, Lola, was one I'd rather not have had, no more than imagining the sexual relations of my own parents.

"Oh, okay, well try to save some time for me," I said.

We both laughed just as Bennett walked up and ex-tended his hand for one last limp shake.

"I wish you the best, Max. If I ever get to Tallahassee, I'll look you up, and I hope when you come to Nashville to visit, you won't be a stranger."

"Sure," I said.

Bennett walked off, and while I appreciated his kind-ness, I knew he was simply doing what he thought he had to do from a political standpoint.

"I've already started working his ass off," Sampson said.

"How?"

"Believe it or not, I've kind of jumped in and noticed some things. We had someone out in the laundry yesterday, and I told him to go help them wash towels, wash cloths, sheets, and pillow cases. He turned as white as the linens, but the little shit went. You should have seen him. I'll bet his Brooks Brothers suit didn't know how to react to all the sweat it soaked up."

"You're joking."

"No, I'm not. That ain't all. I told him I wanted him to stay until seven o'clock in the evening to get a sense of the night shift this week, and then next week, I wanted him to stay around with the night auditor and learn more about that shift. The week after that, I'm going to put him in the kitchen. If he's going to be in management, he's got to get to know the people and every facet of the operation. Know what I mean?"

"Yes, I do. I knew it, and you knew it."

"I suspect he won't last the month, but I could be wrong."

"I hope you're not wrong," I said. "Maybe his family will back off if he quits."

"I doubt it. They're used to hardball, but so am I." Sampson leaned in, cupped his hand, and said, "I've got one hell of a plan." I looked at him, smiled, and he continued, "Earline is on the historic preservation board here in town, and they just elected a new president of the board who just happens to be Bennett's grandmother. That old woman rules the roost. Earline has done got all the old women riled up about saving the hotel, and of course, none of them know what Bennett's family is doing, even old lady Fillmore. She's come out publicly in favor of saving it and now I don't think she would retract her statements. You know, it would be an embarrassment. So, I don't know if they'll offer to sell the land to me, lease it again for a few years until old lady Fillmore is dead and gone, or offer to buy the hotel. Regardless, I'm in much better shape than I was a week or two ago."

"Good for Earline. That's great news."

"Well, there's nothing better than a catfight."

"You may be right. Still, maybe Bennett will just quit."

"I hope he does and then, I'll get someone else. Maybe a young woman. Be better to look at than you or him!" We both laughed.

"You've got a point."

Mr. Sampson gave me a hug, shook my hand, and said, "Good luck, my boy. Don't be a stranger."

"I won't. I appreciate everything." Part of me felt like tears might come, but I held them back. Sampson walked off, and some of the other employees came and either shook hands or hugged me.

Chapter
14

The days following the going-away gathering seemed to go by in slow motion. To save a few dollars, I had decided to attempt packing most of the boxes. I drove over to the liquor store in Green Hills and got boxes out of their dumpster along with a few others from the neighborhood Kroger. Jaden would wrap breakables, I would pack. Jaden would label and tape, and I would move boxes to the garage. Our little system worked nicely.

Moving, it occurred to me, was a two-sided coin. On the one side, there's always the thrill of what awaits the new life, but there's usually a touch of sadness at leaving behind the old life. Jaden and I had been in Nashville for several years, and while we had been in Nashville, we had changed, aged, and so had all the folks back home. In fact, we had traveled home many times for funerals, and it was depressing to me. I remembered one of the last things my grandmother Peacock had said to me. "Max, I wish you lived closer. I just don't get to see ya'll enough."

And, she was right. We didn't get to see each other enough. I had seen her for years growing up, day in and out, and then once I had moved, I was sad that I just couldn't stop by and see her. It made the times we traveled home even more meaningful. Stopping by her house, we'd sit on the porch, drinking chicory coffee and eating a piece of pie she always made when we'd visit. One day I had a strange thought. If I only went home once a year for Christmas, I would probably only see her five or ten more times and that was if she lived another five to ten years. It was an odd sensation, and I think that thought planted a seed deep in my soul. I will go home and if I happen to die in this strange place, I will still be sent home to where my people are. God, please lead me home.

A month later, we were making the trek home to Granny Peacock's funeral and though I did not cry, the lump in my throat could not be swallowed. Jaden knew how hard it was for me and I think it was hard for her, too, because it simply reminded her of her distance from her people, too. And now, packing pictures of family in a box, I am telling them quietly—since Jaden might question my sanity—I don't know if you helped arrange for us to come home, but if you did, thank you. I hate to leave friends and this beautiful land in Tennessee, but thank God, I'm going home again. And I wondered if Granny Peacock had something to do with it.

Though I was a Christian, I don't think I was the Bible-thumping Christian that many professed to be, but I did believe in a spiritual place, where things could line up, and like the magic of Disney, paths could be altered.

I glanced out the window and imagined my grandmother sitting, poised like Mary Poppins, on a cloud and waving at me and I waved.

"Max, what are you waving at?"

"Shooing a fly."

"This box is ready. You look zoned out. Are you okay?"

"Just realizing how close we are to being back home."

"I'm very happy about this, Max, especially since we are going to have a little one."

"Me, too."

Later in the afternoon, Jaden went over to one of her school teacher friend's house for a going-away gathering. The teacher, a dainty, delicate woman named Mame was sweet as could be, and seemed doll-like, but was rather odd. She was several years older than us and had remarried, but hadn't told her own grown children she had remarried. She hadn't even told her mother, according to Jaden, who said it would simply kill her mother to know she'd married again. I thought it strange, but Jaden said when her grown children would come, her new husband would leave the house for a few days until Mame's children had gone. I told Jaden I thought that was *beyond* strange, but what had been hilarious was when her ex-husband found out she was married.

The Orkin man was spraying her ex-husband's house and asked if he was kin to the couple with the same name as his on a certain road. Knowing the road and name—since she had kept her ex-husband's name—he was aware it was his ex-wife's house, but didn't know she had remarried. He was certain she might be living with someone and had called to bless her out and tell her she wasn't living right and she should set a better example for her own children and her students. I thought there was something wrong with the whole story, and it just didn't seem normal, but I saw the humor in it. As soon as I had said it, I could hear Aunt Ophelia, "Don't judge a book by its cover, praise God."

Though Jaden wasn't opposed to my going to the party, no one else had been invited outside the circle of school teachers, and I told Jaden I would prefer to simply rest.

Once Jaden was gone, I laid down in our bedroom and promptly fell asleep. When I awoke, I was thirsty, having apparently slept with my mouth open and it being really dry because of the ceiling fan. I had been asleep for two hours. I turned on the news, looked outside as the sun was setting, and watched the traffic on I-65, and the barges on the Cumberland. Nashville was beautiful, and though I would miss it. I could always come back and visit.

Jaden finally got home shortly after eight o'clock. I was beginning to get concerned, but figured they just couldn't stop talking.

"Sorry, I'm getting in later than I thought. We just talked and had the best time, and guess what they all went in and gave us?"

"What?"

"A $250 gift card to Target."

"That's nice."

"Sure was. We can use it for whatever we want, either for the baby, the move, whatever."

"Well, I think I finished packing everything, and I have my clothes loaded in my Jeep."

"What time are you leaving?"

"Mid-morning some time. I'm in no rush, but I do want to get to Aunt Ophelia's house before dark."

"I'm going to go on to bed."

The next morning, Jaden and I had our last cup of coffee together on the balcony, and I watched the traffic on the Interstate, the barges and tugboats on the Cumberland, and the Nashville skyline, trying to absorb the picture one last time. Nashville, a metropolitan city, was the home of country music, but it would be a bustling place even if not associated with its label of "country music."

I packed some of Jaden's belongings that she would need to prevent her from lifting anything to her car when she arrived in a couple of days, and we kissed and hugged good-bye. I was on the Interstate by eleven and drove without stopping until I was past Atlanta, and even then, I pulled off the road long enough to fill up with gas, get a diet Coke and a pack of cashews. Jaden and I talked briefly by cell phone. She mainly wanted to see if I was making good time or not.

I listened to The Traveling Wilburys at least twice. I also listened to some older CD's I owned. Tom T. Hall, Joe South, and Emmylou Harris—who I jokingly told Jaden I would run away with if she ever invited me. I loved her voice and her natural look. Jaden told me to go ahead, that I might get a BMW after all.

I finally pulled in to Aunt Ophelia's about dusk. The peacocks were down in the woods, screaming, and I called Mama and Daddy to let them know I was there in case any locals decided to call them and tell them a strange vehicle was at Aunt Ophelia's. I unpacked, got organized, and decided to get a good night's sleep before I started to work the next morning at the Apalachee. I also decided I would clean and rearrange Ophelia's furniture around, so we'd have room for some of our things, even though most of it would end up in a secured storage facility in Tallahassee, but that work could wait a day or two.

The next day, the drive to Tallahassee wasn't bad at all. It took about forty-five minutes, and the more I thought about it, the more it occurred to me that Jaden often had a forty-five minute commute with traffic in Nashville. I met the doorman, Jack, who was Effie's cousin. He was kind, and I could tell by their eyes they were related. It's funny how you can tell these little things, and of course, I don't know if I would have made the connection if I hadn't known. I filled out human resources paperwork related to social security, health care, and so forth, and Ms. Lola came and welcomed me officially to the Apalachee. We toured the facility again, but this time I was introduced to every employee on the property who was at work. Given there were three shifts, some employees I would have to meet later.

Finally, Lola looked at her watch. "Max, I can't believe it's lunch already. We should grab a bite. I'll bet you're starving."

"No, not really," I responded. "I didn't even realize the time."

We walked to the café, took seats, and ordered salads. Lola explained that I could charge breakfast, lunch and dinner anytime I wanted and they would either deduct it from my paycheck, or I could simply pay it. She said she'd only be stiffed once in all the years she had owned the place. Lola talked a little about her family, and particularly her husband's decline, and I was surprised when she shifted the conversation to my family.

"Max, I knew some of your family."

"What do you mean?"

"First, my uncle was engaged to your Aunt Ophelia. They met in the restaurant here at the Apalachee. She was a beautiful woman, very regal. I remember imitating her as a child. I knew your grandparents, too, but not well, and I remember your Great Aunt Helen."

"That's amazing," I said. "I wondered why you asked me if I would commute or live here when you hired me."

"Yes, I think we went to your family farm once. I remember a pond, the old bungalow, the peacocks."

"What happened to your uncle?"

"He was killed in a car accident."

"So, then, that means he was Ophelia's first fiancé. She was engaged to two other men, both of whom died. One with the flu in the epidemic and one in the Korean War."

"That sounds right. They loved to go for rides in his convertible Thunderbird, and I remember him telling her they would always be together."

Part of me wondered about the mysterious rider, the logger who hit aunt Ophelia claimed he saw the day she was killed. It's easier to imagine it to be true than try to investigate it, but part of me felt like calling him over in Waycross where he lived to ask him what the fellow looked like, but I figured it would make a better story to tell. "And you knew my great Aunt Helen?"

"Vaguely. There was something wrong with her. It seemed to get worse from what I recall, but you know adults didn't talk about things like that much back then and certainly not around children."

"What were her symptoms?"

"She was brilliant, very quiet, but she could make predictions. I remember her telling me I would one day own and run this hotel, and I was fascinated by that thought. Of course, I was just a child and it didn't take much to fascinate me then. But I do recall that my uncle bought a lot of oil stock from her prediction and hit the jackpot. I also think your grandparents did, too. In fact, there were some men from Washington who came here to talk with her and your grandparents shortly after they did that. I think they suspected something fishy. She began to suspect everyone. I don't think she was outright paranoid, but she was walking a thin line. She was truly a mystery, but she did begin to tell people things that upset them, and once in a while, there was a scene at the hotel. I think your grandparents finally decided to send her for some rest and relaxation at a new facility. I don't really know what happened to her after that, and of course, Max, this is all from a child's perspective many years ago."

"Apparently, I read in an old letter in a trunk that she was given a prefrontal lobotomy and died a year later at the state hospital in Milledgeville."

"That's sad. I don't know that she ever told anything that wasn't true. Looking back, it was as if she had a sixth sense, an intuition, and she could read people very well. If she told people the truth, even at the hospital, then people wouldn't have liked that."

"True. I guess it's too long ago to check it all out now, and I'm sure there would be no records. Plus, most of the people who would have known something about it would probably be deceased. Anyway, that is amazing. You have helped me more today than you'll ever know. Thanks."

"Well, what are you and Jaden going to name this little girl?"

"Ophelia, but maybe we'll give her the middle name of Helen."

"I think that would be splendid."

Our conversation was interrupted by her cell phone ringing. Her caller was the hospice nurse telling her that Mr. Smith's breathing had become somewhat labored, and she should come home. I asked if she was okay, and she replied, "You're never really ready to let go, but you have to."

Chapter
15

L ola's husband held on for a few more months, and I could tell by her eyes at the hotel that his suffering was taking a toll on her, too. When he finally passed one rainy Thursday afternoon, one of the clerks handed me a note with the message. I went to the Human Resources office and ask them to order flowers and to post a notice to all employees.

I also decided I would call Mimi Ciucevich and cancel our appointment to look at a house in the Vineyard, though I had been excited to see this particular house. There was something about the rolling hills of Tallahassee that had an old world feel, but when I came across a golf course subdivision built around a wine vineyard near Monticello, I did fall in love. There hadn't been an opening in that area, and there still wasn't.

Lola's sister Mimi knew everyone in Tallahassee, but she looked nothing like Lola. She was heavy, had platinum blonde hair, wore lots of make-up, wore a ring on every finger, and drove a convertible Mercedes. Lola was much more unassuming. Mimi had married a popular local psychologist who basically knew most of the secrets of Tallahassee society and he, too, had made a killing as a businessman on the side. Mimi had made some money from real estate through the years as well and she had connections.

She found a couple who had recently retired and were thinking of moving over to Orange Park, near Jacksonville, to be near their children. They were thinking of listing their home at the Vineyards, but were very particular and peculiar. They agreed to show us the place, but with the visitation and funeral, I assumed it might be wiser to wait until Sunday to see the place. When I called Mimi, she recognized the wisdom of that decision. I asked if she felt there was anything we could do for Lola, and she said no.

I called Jaden, who had been having a lot of discomfort in the Georgia heat and humidity. "Jaden, Lola's husband finally passed."

"Do you know the arrangements?"

"I think they'll have the visitation and say the rosary tomorrow night, and the funeral will be on Saturday."

"I'll let our parents know, but I doubt mine will go. Yours might go."

"What are you doing?"

"Laying here, thinking. What else can I do. I feel like a cow. If I go outside, I feel like I'm going to topple over and get eaten by the damned gnats."

"I understand."

"No, Max, you don't understand. I don't mean to be mean, but you don't understand."

"Okay, then, do you need anything?"

"No."

"Do you want me to bring home some supper?"

"Get yourself something. I obviously don't need to eat."

"You do need to keep up your strength for the baby."

"Well, then, just bring whatever."

"Oh, I canceled the appointment this afternoon to see the house at the Vineyards."

"Good. I don't feel like it anyway."

"Maybe this weekend we can see it."

"Maybe."

I told Jaden I loved her, and she hung up. I feel sure she was miserable and part of me just felt bad that no matter what I said or tried to do, she was still going to be miserable, and

she looked it, too. Everything had spread. Her face, nose, behind, hips, etc. She would get up and walk by a mirror and
cry, and I must admit that I had seen Demi Moore in a magazine pregnant, mostly nude, and she looked pretty good, but
Jaden didn't. I wouldn't have told her that, of course. And
while I did miss sex, there were ways to gratify oneself,
which I did discreetly in the shower, and vowed never to discuss it, given the taboo nature of the act, and while one typically looks at some magazine or imagines something erotic
while doing it, fundamentalists believed to imagine sex with
another is to have done it—kind of like President Carter had
lusted in his heart. So, naturally, I felt like I was going to hell,
and while I probably could hear Aunt Ophelia saying something, I shut her out of my mind completely.

   The next evening, Mama, Daddy, Jaden and I loaded
into my Jeep to attend the visitation. There were quite a few
vehicles at the funeral home, and when we got inside, we all
signed the register. I saw Lola talking with a couple of employees, probably about the funeral service the next day, and
I heard the organ music playing softly in the background.
Since there was no sign of an organ or organist, I assumed it
was piped in. We walked over and stood by the closed casket
to look at a display of photos from Howard Smith's earlier
life including a photo with a platoon in Viet Nam. The young
soldiers stood in fatigues, shirtless and dog tags hanging on
their bare chests. They were all smiling; some propped guns
on their black boots and others seemed less relaxed. I wondered how many had survived. Another photo showed Howard in his Seminole football uniform at Florida State along
side Burt Reynolds, one of their more famous players. To me,
the nicest photos were the ones of Howard and Lola—their
marriage, a beach trip, where he was obviously lifting her in
the air, a painting party at their home, and him in childhood.
A picture of him and a grandfather, I supposed, with a string
of fish, one with an old woman, a grandmother with horned-
rimmed glasses shelling peas in a front porch swing, him with
siblings or cousins after a romp in a mud puddle. The memories made, the time passed, and now his life had ended. I

glanced at Jaden who was talking about her pregnancy with a couple of ladies from the Apalachee, and Mama and Daddy were talking with someone I didn't know, but Mama signaled me over.

"Max, this is my distant cousin on my mama's side, Will Rewis."

We shook hands, and I told him it was nice to meet him. His skin was dark and wrinkled and his hair was completely white. His eyes were deep set, and his cheekbones were high.

"We went to school together at Pavo High," Will said.

"Pavo High?" I had not heard of it.

"Well, back then we had a high school, which is what the elementary school is now," Mama said. "Me and Will might have got married if your Daddy hadn't come along."

"I thought ya'll were cousins," I said.

"Not close enough that it would have mattered."

Somehow I found the conversation going somewhere I didn't want to go. "Well, no offense, but I'm glad Daddy came along or else I might not be here."

They all chuckled, and I moved over to the flowers. I noticed folks coming in, kneeling on the prayer bench, but I wanted to see what the wreath the hotel had sent looked like. I felt odd reading the cards, but found it rather quickly. It was a nice spray with summer flowers including different variety of lilies. I thought it ought to be nice for what we'd ended up paying the florists. Somehow, florists had become the socially acceptable way to show respect through the years and due to that belief, they had become quite wealthy arranging cut flowers and sticking them in green Styrofoam. Funeral home owners, too, had become quite wealthy through the years with their smooth talking sales tactics to people during one of the most vulnerable times in their lives.

I finally found Lola was free from the crowd. I walked up and told her I was sorry.

"Max, thank you for coming."

"I'm very sorry."

"I know you are and Mimi said you'd offered to help. Right now, I don't need anything, but I might be scarce for a few days until I get some things resolved."

"No need to worry."

"I may need your help, however. I do have some things that I'd either like for you to have or send to Goodwill or Salvation Army. Do you think you might give me a call in a few days and stop by and have a look? Howard even mentioned your having them."

"I will be glad to."

"Jaden should have stayed home. She looks miserable."

"Oh, she really is."

"It was great meeting your parents. You look like your dad."

"I don't know if that's good or bad."

We both chuckled, Lola stepped forward, hugged me and said, "Thanks for coming," then stepped away.

When we walked out to my Jeep and got in, Mama said, "What in the world was that bench for that people kept kneeling on?"

"I think it's called a prayer bench. Catholics have those."

"Well, I just couldn't be a Catholic. My knees just couldn't take it. It's a good thing I'm Baptist."

I smiled to myself and pulled onto Highway 319 North. I asked Jaden how she was feeling.

"I'm okay."

"Ya'll feel like riding by that house in the Vineyards?"

"Sure," Mama said. "Can we go in?"

"No, they are still there. They haven't even listed it, but Mimi knows them and says they are thinking of moving closer to their children since they retired."

"They ought to make their kids move closer to them, like ya'll did," Mama said.

"Not everybody can just up and do that," Daddy responded.

"I'm up for it," Jaden added.

I turned onto Capitol Circle, the city loop, which took us over toward the Monticello Road. We had to backtrack a little bit because I had already headed toward Thomasville.

"Hey, Jaden. Do you see what's coming up on your right?"

"Yum. I could go for a DQ blizzard."

"Ice cream would be nice," said Mama.

"We'll swing in there on the way back."

"Well, here we are," I said.

"Oh, I like this," Mama said. "The homes are nice and I love all the grape vines. And they make wine."

"Yeah, they have a wine shop here at the Golf club. Of course, they actually make the wine and have more vineyards elsewhere."

"You ever had any of their wine?" Daddy asked.

"Not that I recall."

"Well, if you moved here, you'd have to put up with traffic and a lot of neighbors. You can stay at Ophelia's place free."

"I know," I said. "But we can get away on weekends and come up there."

As we drove down the hills and up the hills through the vineyard and golf course, we turned down a side road. The house rested at the end of the street and the view from the backyard was vineyards and the ninth hole with a small pond. The house was a modern Tudor-style with a stone entrance, brick, and siding. The circular drive and drive going into the side garage was concrete with brick inlay, which was stunning. The couple was outside clipping roses in the side yard, and though it was dusk, there was enough light out to see.

"I would like to see inside," Jaden said. "I love the outside."

"Me, too," Mama said. "You were mad about the other contracts falling through, but if you get this, you won't give a damn."

"Mama," I said. "Did you say damn?"

"Yes, I did. Pull over and tell them who you are and see if we can go in."

I pulled the Jeep to the curb, got out, and walked over to them. I introduced myself, told them how sorry I was we had to cancel due to Lola's husband's passing and my wife not feeling well, and they said they understood, didn't mind, and for Jaden and my parents to feel free to get out, come in, and look around.

After much small talk, when Southerners are looking for some sort of a connection, Jaden finally realized one of John and Theresa Myers' daughters was a friend of hers in college. Mr. Myers had helped develop the Vineyards and he had been on the design team of an architectural firm, where he had designed the capitol building, several projects at Florida State University, and redesigned many other buildings downtown, along with several other projects around the Southeast. Myers pulled me aside and asked, "What do you think of the capitol building?"

"It looks nice. I haven't actually been inside it."

"You think it looks like male genitals?"

"I hadn't thought of it, though I had heard that somewhere."

"We did it that way on purpose because of all the pricks working there. We thought it fitting." Myers guffawed, and he was one of those hardened characters who you couldn't figure out if he was joking or not.

Mrs. Myers, walking with Jaden, Mama and Daddy inside, yelled back over her shoulder: "Don't you believe a word he says. He hasn't told the truth since before we were married."

Mr. Myers changed the subject. "Max, I was here everyday when they built this house. I made them use real ply board, not pressed board, I put thirty-five year shingles on the roof, and the wood floors are solid oak that I hand picked. It's a solid house. I about drove the contractor crazy, but that happens when you got an engineer building a house."

"That's great," I said. "More people should be like that."

"I agree. Come on in," he said.

The house inside was beautiful. The floors had apparently several layers of polyurethane. I liked the light fixtures, the cabinets in the kitchen, the wooden shutters throughout the house, the spacious rooms, the nine-foot ceilings in all the rooms, and the crown molding. It was a beautiful place, and Jaden and I looked at each other and smiled. We knew this was the house, if they were going to sell.

We were all standing in the living room and I said,

"Well, we would certainly be interested if ya'll decide to sell."

"We should know in a few days," Mrs. Myers said. "We'll let Mimi know."

"That would be great," I said.

Jaden had a funny look and grabbed her abdomen. "Mind if I sit down? I'm not feeling too good."

"No, honey, not at all." Mrs. Myers and Mama walked Jaden to a leather chair.

"You okay, Jaden?" I asked.

"I don't know. I'm embarrassed," she said. Mama was fanning her and Mrs. Myers brought her a glass of water. The drive, the funeral home visitation, the house tour, and probably the stairs in particular, had most likely been too much for Jaden. She'd overdone it, as usual. Mr. Myers and Daddy were talking, and I was keeping my attention focused on Jaden while Mama and Mrs. Myers doted over her. Jaden said something to Mama and Mrs. Myers, but I couldn't quite make it out, and she began to cry.

"Oh dear," Mama said.

"I'll get some paper towels," Mrs. Myers said.

"What is it?"

Mama whispered to me, "I think she tee-teed a little in her pants."

Mrs. Myers came back, handed Mama the paper towels, and told Jaden, "Honey, it'll be okay. It's not going to mess up this chair." Jaden scooted up a little, and Mama dabbed the chair and when she pulled the paper towels back, they were red.

"Jaden, you're bleeding," Mama said. "Max, call an ambulance."

"No," Jaden said. "I'm fine. We can just drive over to the hospital."

"No, Jaden. You don't need to worry, but something might be torn. Sit back."

Mrs. Myers brought a stool over and made Jaden prop up her legs. I dialed 911 and told them my wife was eight months pregnant and had begun to bleed a little. I felt like we needed to take her to the hospital. I had to ask for the address, which I'm sure made the 911 operator suspicious, and I guess I felt like explaining why we were there, but she said it was okay. She told me the ambulance would be there shortly, that they were enroute. I paced and held Jaden's hand. I was concerned about Jaden, but I was concerned about the baby, too.

The first to arrive was the fire department. I walked outside and said, "I called for an ambulance." One of the firemen ignored me, but the other said, "We respond, too, until the ambulance can get here. We're closer."

"Okay," I said as they sprinted into the house. I could hear another siren in the background, and neighbors began to shuffle onto their porches to see what was going on. It occurred to me they might think something was wrong with Mr. or Mrs. Myers, and I felt like someone should reassure them their neighbors weren't dying. Within two minutes, the ambulance came rushing down the lane, and the paramedics opened the side doors on the ambulance and brought in suitcases with equipment. When they had ascertained the situation, one of them said, "Ms. Peacock, we need to get you to the hospital. Do you have a preference?"

"My doctor is affiliated with TCH," Jaden said. Jaden's vitals were okay, except for an elevated blood pressure, probably from the tension and anxiety. One EMT returned with a stretcher on wheels, and they picked her up and loaded Jaden onto it, wheeling her back out to the waiting vehicle. I asked if I could ride in the ambulance with them and they said told me it was a liability issue. I told Mr. and Mrs. Myers I was sorry, and they reassured me all would be okay and that we'd talk soon. Mama, Daddy and I climbed in the Jeep and waited for the ambulance to take off. When it did, we followed close behind.

On the way to the hospital, I gave Mama my cell phone and she called Jaden's parents, told them what was going on, and suggested they meet us at Tallahassee Community Hospital. Though the emergency room was packed, they rolled Jaden right back into an area and pulled the curtain. The EMT's spoke to the nurse and she began to check Jaden's vitals again. The nurse told me they were going to try and find her a room on the maternity ward, and they would notify her physician. Daddy just stood in a corner and looked around while Mama sat on the edge of Jaden's bed rubbing her head with a wet cloth.

It took about an hour before they moved Jaden to a room, and by then, her parents had arrived. Her doctor stopped by shortly after, asked us to leave the room while she examined Jaden. A few minutes later, the nurse stepped outside and told us we could come back in.

The doctor looked at me. "Jaden has placenta privia, which is an uncommon complication that can cause excessive bleeding before or during delivery. Soon after conception, the placenta begins to form and provides oxygen and nutrients to your growing baby and removes waste products from your baby's blood. It attaches both to the wall of your uterus and to your baby's umbilical cord, forming a vital connection between you and your baby." The doctor continued, and sort of gestured in the air with his hands, which I thought odd. "Early in pregnancy, the placenta can implant in the lower part of the uterus. As the uterus grows, the placenta usually moves away from the opening of the uterus. If it doesn't, the cervix may be blocked. The placenta is beginning to detach from the lower part of the uterus as the cervix begins to open before labor. It can cause severe bleeding, but you got here in plenty of time that Jaden, nor the baby, is in harm's way at this point."

"Praise the Lord," said Mama.

"Well, what does all this mean, exactly?" I asked. Nothing like a doctor to speak to an audience in scientific language that no amount of gesturing in the air is going to make a group of laymen understand.

"I'd like to perform an ultrasound," he said, "and you all are welcome to watch, if Jaden doesn't mind."

"No, I don't mind," Jaden said.

"I think everything is fine, but I want to keep you overnight. If the baby's heartbeat is elevated or your vitals are off, I might want to go ahead and induce. You would be a few weeks early, but everything should be okay with the baby, and I don't know that I would want to risk jeopardizing the baby anymore than we already have."

"Thank you," said Jaden, and I nodded at the doctor.

"Okay, then. We'll get to the ultrasound and go from there."

Jaden's mom had taken over the cold cloth dampening of Jaden's forehead and the hand holding while Mama looked on. Our fathers sat in the two recliners in the hospital room, which they refer to as a birthing suite. While it was a rather large room, with only one single hospital bed, there wasn't anything in the room that would lead one to think of the room as a birthing suite. Hospital tile, nice, soothing wallpaper, and a closet-like bathroom with shower in addition to the bed and recliners were the sum. Of course, there was the standard oxygen insert in the wall above the bed.

Our parents had not seen the ultrasound, and when Jaden and I had been born, there were no ultrasounds, so our parents didn't really know what to expect. We had showed them the CD they made for us in the first months, and while they had shown excitement, no one could really tell that the little blob floating around was a child. It looked more like a turtle.

I stood next to Jaden and held her hand when they squirted the jelly-like substance onto her belly and the doctor began to roll the microphone-looking monitor around her belly. Finally, he found the baby. No longer was there a little turtle, but the baby looked fully-developed, and our parents were surprised. Our mothers began to cry with excitement, and Daddy said, "Well, I'll be. Would you look at that?" Just as we were watching, one of the feet pressed against Jaden's belly, and we could all see the footprint on her skin. Even I was amazed at that, but for some reason, the image of alien movies popped into my mind.

None of us were paying attention to the vital signs on the monitor, having been too busy focusing on the baby, but the doctor informed us the heartbeat was too fast and the baby was showing signs of distress. "I would like to move ahead with a C-section in just a bit. I'm going to have the nurse start an epidural. This will regionally numb you for the C-section so you can be awake for the delivery."

"No," Jaden said. "I don't want a C-section."

"Jaden, a natural birth in this case just isn't going to be possible. You have placenta privia. The baby may not survive the natural birth, and right now, the baby is showing signs of distress. We need to move on."

"But I really didn't want a scar." The doctor looked at me and smirked.

"Jaden, this isn't about you and a scar. It's about our baby."

Jaden began to whimper, but her mother comforted her, and the doctor said he was going to prepare for surgery. None of us had expected such a drastic turn of events, and we all felt lucky it had gone as well as it had, given the circumstances. When the anesthetist arrived to insert the epidural, I was somewhat nauseated watching them insert the needle into her back, and because she claimed some discomfort, she didn't show much reaction. Nurses kept coming in and checking her vitals as well as the baby's vitals, and all seemed stable to me, though I certainly didn't know much.

After a while, a team came to get her. They carefully lifted Jaden and put her in a new bed. One nurse held scrubs and asked if I planned to be in the room.

Jaden heard this, and answered for me. "Yes." Then she turned toward me. "Max, I want you in there."

"Okay," I said when I had never been comfortable with any sort of blood. My typical reaction would be to freeze and space out. Whether this comes from having been cut and having stitches several times or seeing splattered road kill along the highways, I don't know.

I put on the scrubs over my clothes and walked with them as they rolled Jaden down a hallway into a small operating room. I just stood next to Jaden holding her hand closer to where her head lay on the bed. They put up a curtain around the area they cut, and I saw tugging of skin while the doctor and nurse braced the bed to keep it from moving though the wheels were locked. It was somehow disgusting to me and

Jaden, oblivious to the pain, smiled and hummed a song that I could not make out. Within minutes, they pulled the baby out and up in the air. She flailed and began to scream out a small cry which I thought was beautiful. They cut the cord, tied it off, wiped off the baby, wrapped her in a little blanket and handed her to Jaden. She was beautiful.

Jaden cried with happiness. I then noticed the doctor laying some other things on a tray, which mainly looked like skin and blood. They sewed Jaden's abdomen, which was another joy to watch and cleaned as best they could, removing the curtain, the blood-soaked blanket and cloths, and putting a new blanket atop Jaden.

"Isn't she just precious?" Jaden asked the nurse.

"Yes," the nurse said. She added, "We need to clean her up, weigh her, put a bracelet on her, and get her in the incubator. Do you all have a name?"

"Ophelia Helen," I said.

"What a beautiful name," she commented, taking little Ophelia over to a tiny table with a light. She placed her under the warm light on the little bed that resembled a shoebox and Ophelia squinted and looked around and she would open her mouth and make "waaa" sounds that weren't really cries, but I supposed just noise. I stood next to her and realized how vulnerable babies really are. I looked into her eyes and they were small, tadpole-like dark eyes. I would look at her, let her hold my finger and make little chirping noises, and I imagined she looked at me and wondered what I was, who I was, and actually if she would have asked, I'm not sure I could have answered anymore. I was a father and now Jaden was a mother and our parents had become grandparents and I didn't know what that meant. Soon, they had Ophelia tagged and moved into the nursery and our parents stood by the window looking in, talking about how beautiful their granddaughter was. Other parents and grandparents stood by the window admiring their own, and I thought this had to be one of the more special times in life that doesn't last very long at all.

When I got back to the hospital room, Jaden was fresher looking, but exhausted. She had new bedding and the blanket was tucked under her legs to prevent movement, I suppose. I sat at the edge of her bed, took Jaden's hand, and said, "She is a beautiful little girl."

Jaden smiled. "They'll bring her in a little bit for me to breastfeed. You want to watch and learn?"

I smiled. "I know I've gained a little weight with you, but I don't think I'm quite there yet." Our dads laughed and Jaden smiled.

"Why don't you go get a bite to eat, then? I'll rest a while."

Dad, Jaden's dad, and I went down to the café at the hospital, got a sandwich and talked for a while. I was tired, as were they, but I'm sure we weren't as tired as Jaden. When we returned to the room, Jaden was asleep, and Mama was nodding.

"Jaden's mom is going to spend the night tonight," Mama whispered. "So, let's get on home and you can come back first thing."

"Max?" I turned. Jaden had stirred. "Go on home. Mom's going to spend the night with me. I'll see you in the morning. Will you pack some of my things?"

"Sure, but what about Ophelia?"

"She has to spend the night, too."

"I know that, but is she okay in there by herself?"

"Yes, she'll be okay." I turned to go. "Oh, and Max. Will you call the Myers and let them know and also that we want their house? Also, call Mame."

"Okay, get some rest." I leaned in and kissed Jaden's forehead.

Everyone said goodbye, and her parents hugged me and said congratulations. Mama, Daddy and I went back to the nursery and stood watching little Ophelia. I was struck by her beauty and not just because she was my child. Her dark fuzzy hair, olive skin, that was both olive and red from the birth trauma, were striking, and I hoped I would live long enough to see her grow to be the helping soul I imagined she might be. I was also struck by the miracle of birth.

"Well, I imagine as good looking as she is, she'll put a

little gray in that hair of yours or you'll lose it one," Daddy said.

I laughed. "Don't think she'll ever go out on a date without me going with her."

"Ya'll see that?" Mama asked, pointing.

"What?" I asked.

"She's got a little birthmark on her leg just like Ophelia had. How 'bout that?"

"Well, I'll be. Sure does," Daddy said.

"Genes are an amazing thing," I said, smiling. Part of me could hear Aunt Ophelia in my head. "You finally got something right, praise God."